Dare to Dream

Portraits of Love
Book 1

Dare to Dream

Portraits of Love
Book 1

KAREN ROSSI

A Karen Rossi Romance

Wisteria Publications

Wisteria Publications
507-4 Briar Hill Heights
New Tecumseth, ON
L9R 1Z7

Dare to Dream
ISBN: 978-1-988763-07-1
Copyright © 2017 by Kaarina Brooks

Published in Canada 2017

Layout and Cover Art by Taria van Weesenbeek

Please contact the author at brooks.kaarina@gmail.com for any questions or comments.

Dedication

This book is dedicated to my sister, Raili: my brain-storming buddy, my nit-picky editor, and my painfully honest critic. We have been writing together since childhood, and hope never to stop creating. Without Raili's support, writing wouldn't be any fun.

Other Books by Karen Rossi

"Portraits of Love" Series
    Dare to Love
    Dare to Surrender
    Dare to Trust

Despite Everything
Beyond Forgiveness
No Home for My Heart

Acknowledgements

I want to thank Taria van Weesenbeek who has given so generously of her time to bring this novel to life.

Chapter One

"Wow! This I like."

Shaylee Palmer did a three-sixty and took a quick survey of the work on display in the foyer of The Four Winds Gallery.

This was her kind of art. Much preferable to that abstract stuff.

"Thanks, Grandpa," she whispered, "for making all this possible."

She walked toward a painting set up on an easel in the middle of the floor but came to an abrupt halt when a tight male voice asked, "Can I help you?" The way one would address an unwelcome intruder, while trying to remain polite.

Shaylee pivoted around to see a short, balding man at the door of an office on the left. She gave a quick, nervous laugh. "No, thank you, I'm just looking." She knew her unfashionable winter jacket and boots made it very clear she wouldn't be in the market for an expensive painting. He probably thought she'd just come in to warm herself.

Still, he honoured her with a pinched smile. "I'm Max Storm, the proprietor. If you have any questions, please ask."

Please ask? Hah! He looked down his nose at her like he fully expected her to meekly leave before she tracked mud on his carpets.

"Thanks, I will," Shaylee muttered. She felt like stringing him along for a while, asking about the prices, but he probably wouldn't appreciate such nonsense. He'd already dismissed her as a potential client by turning his back on her and returning to his office.

Shaylee shrugged. Someday Mr. High and Mighty might hang *her* art on these very walls.

She entered the first room to her right and then slowly negotiated her way through the small, tastefully laid-out inner galleries, the clomp of her heavy winter boots muffled by carpets. Some of the rooms had photographs, others had oils, and in one gallery were sculptures of—she nodded with approval—totally recognizable humans, or parts thereof.

As Shaylee entered another gallery, she halted and her hand flew to her mouth. What beautiful paintings. Whose work was this? A promo on the wall told her the name of the artist, his birth date, as well as the particulars of his quite prestigious artistic career.

Michael Merrick. Such a young man to be already so well recognized in the art world, with a room devoted entirely to his work. She circled around, inspecting each picture in turn. It was as if she'd entered an enchanted world. Back and forth she wandered, taking in the paintings close up, and then stepping back a few paces, returning to each, again and again. One winter scene particularly engrossed her, and she lost track of time as she stood admiring it.

"You like it?"

The deep male voice startled her from her reverie and she whirled around to face a broad chest. The mouth that had asked the question was considerably higher and, as she looked up, she thought she saw golden lights dance in a pair of brown eyes.

Golden lights dancing? Was that possible?

"I love it. It's my favourite of all these wonderful paintings here." Shaylee swung her arms to encompass the entire room. "These are absolutely the best I've seen. I've been here for probably half an hour," she glanced at her watch to verify the statement, "just drinking them in."

A glint of laughter in the man's eyes made her squirm inside. He probably thought her praise was way over the top. One of her unfortunate tendencies, but she really meant it.

The man rubbed his strong chin. "So, why do you like that one in particular?"

The five-o-clock shadow made him so attractive in a very masculine way, Shaylee had to force herself to jerk her gaze away from him. She turned instead to the wintry forest scene that had so absorbed her. "I find it incredible the way the luminous sunlight filters through the branches onto the pristine, sapphire snow. I wish I knew how the artist did it. Beautiful, don't you agree?"

The man only nodded.

"Funny thing is, the artist," she pointed to the signature scrawled on the painting, "Michael Merrick's his name—probably doesn't even know himself how he got that glowing effect."

The man quirked a questioning eyebrow. "Oh? How's that?" Deep dimples in his cheeks signaled his amusement at her comment.

As Shaylee watched, the smile crept up from his mouth, and when it reached his eyes the golden lights were there again. Dancing. Fascinating. So it hadn't just been her imagination.

She smiled in return, hoping to keep those dimples from disappearing. In her twenty-four years of life she'd come to acknowledge her fondness for men with dimples.

"Well," she mused. "I read somewhere a great painter may know a lot about painting, but then he'll do something and wonder how he got that effect. You know," she pointed at the glowing snow, "that could have been just a happy mistake."

Now the man laughed. The full sound from deep inside his chest made Shaylee grin.

"So you think the light on the snow was a happy mistake, do you?"

"Well, maybe not," she conceded. "But however he did it, it's absolutely fantastic. The hues are so clear and vivid. The snow is . . . it's perfectly scintillating."

The man looked down at her, surprise on his face.

Shaylee frowned. "Don't you agree?" Probably she was too effusive again. "Foot-in-the-mouth disease" her family back home called it.

"I guess that's the magic of water colours," he said, not answering her directly.

But, as usual, having got started, Shaylee couldn't contain her eagerness. "It's as though this painter looks at the world through eyes that see everything in a vibrant, optimistic light. He must be a wonderful person."

"I assume you paint?" He failed to join in her effusive praises of the artist.

Shaylee sighed. "Yes, but I've only dabbled on my own. I'm just getting settled here in Toronto and I'd love to find an art class somewhere." And discover if what she'd been doing at home was any good. Had Grandpa been right when he'd praised her artistic talent, or had he only been kind to his only granddaughter? He was gone now and would never know if what he said was true, but the small endowment he'd left her was making it possible for her to find out the truth.

"Did you happen to see the brochures over there?" The man indicated a low table on which some papers were scattered.

Shaylee picked one up and quickly perused it. Art classes. A business card was attached to each application form.

Michael Merrick

Cordova, Laine and Merrick

Triple M Graphic Design and Production

"Michael Merrick?" she cried with delight. "Hey! *That's my artist.*"

The man's face broke into a wide grin and Shaylee had to reciprocate as she looked up at him. Ah, those dimples.

"Yeah," he said. "And looks like your artist has a day job, too, besides giving art lessons. Busy fellow."

She nodded. "I guess that's an artist's life for you. Even though his paintings are so wonderful, he has to work at other things to make ends meet." She slipped the brochure into the large tote bag she carried over one shoulder. "So, do you take lessons?"

"Lessons?" He hesitated. "No, I don't."

Shaylee thought she could hear a tinge of bitterness in his voice as he added, "But I probably should."

With her head, Shaylee pointed toward the brochures on the table. "There's your chance. Judging by his work, I'd say this Michael Merrick knows what he's doing. I'm sure you'd find him helpful."

"Actually, I—"

The proprietor popped his bald head into the room. "Mike, can I— oh, sorry, I didn't mean to interrupt."

Shaylee hitched her tote bag higher onto her shoulder. "That's all right. I was just leaving, anyway." With a wave she turned to go. Bye, Mike. Too bad her chances of ever meeting this good-looking guy again were about zero. Or less.

She stepped through the open glass doors and set off briskly down the sidewalk. The March afternoon was sunny, and spring was making valiant stabs at the stubborn winter, creating slushy piles of dirty snow along the curbs. Strolling in this old part of Toronto, Shaylee felt like she was on a totally different planet from her home on the farm near Kitchener. She loved it here. The streets were lined with huge, skeletal trees which now, without their lush summer foliage, allowed an intimate peek at the redbrick century homes. Many of these grand old houses, with their white, ornate scrollwork, had been transformed into chic boutiques and unique galleries, like The Four Winds, where she'd met that charming, dimpled Mike.

A sparkle of sunlight dancing on the melting snow made her think of his eyes. Impulsively she turned to look back, hoping to see a glimpse of him. Of course he was nowhere in sight.

Mike. Knowing his name was like a thin thread of hope that maybe, just maybe, they could meet again. After all, how many Mikes could there be in a city of five million? She smiled to herself.

As she waited for the "Walk" sign, she thought back to the rather stuffy proprietor of The Four Winds Gallery. Wouldn't it be something if one day her paintings hung on those walls, right alongside Michael Merrick's? Would people be as impressed with her work as she was with his?

Shaylee knew she was good. After all, everyone back home always praised her work to the skies. And dear, dear Grandfather had practically crowned her the Canadian Michelangelo. But did any of these people know what real art was—any more than she did herself? She'd only painted what was there around her home—the picturesque countryside and the lake nearby. Certainly nothing resembling the strange lines and splashes of colour she'd seen in some of the galleries she'd visited. If that was real art, she was missing it by a country mile. She only hoped art connoisseurs wouldn't judge her realistic work as simply *very nice* efforts of some dilettante.

The problem was, she'd never had the nerve to get a professional opinion of her paintings. What if they said she wasn't any good? She'd rather keep hoping and dreaming than face the possibility of disappointment. But maybe, if she went to these art classes and if she worked like a demon to show Michael Merrick what she was capable of doing, he might simply fall all over himself praising her, and tell her she was incredibly talented.

Hah! Dream on, girl. Didn't pride goeth before the fall, or something like that? Because, instead of praising her, he might pat her on the head and say her paintings were *very nice*. Like her loving big brothers, who'd told her Auntie Grace would be thrilled to receive one of her pictures for Christmas.

Nice. What a horrid word! Shaylee's heart sank and her shoulders sagged. That would surely kill her dream of becoming a recognized artist. And then what would she do? Go home with her tail between her legs, back to working at the florist shop?

No way! She hadn't come this far in order to let self-doubts stop her.

Standing at the curb, she rummaged through her bag and brought out the brochure. A set of ten art classes would start in a couple of weeks and—happy surprise!—they would be held an easy bus ride from where she lived in the north end of the city.

She threw back her shoulders and scowled defiantly at the glowing red hand that tried to block her path. She'd come to Toronto to forge ahead and succeed. Failure was *not* on her agenda.

The "Walk" signal appeared, right on cue.

Shaylee got off the bus and strolled slowly along the sidewalk, searching the front of each building for number fifty-eight. She'd wanted to find the art studio ahead of time during daylight hours, so she wouldn't have to search for it in the dark on the first night of class.

There it was. The rusty metal numbers looked ready to fall off the top of the narrow door. The brochure had said the studio was located on the second floor, above a fruit market, and so it was. Beside the narrow door was the store's picture window, displaying a bewildering assortment of colourful fruits and flowers.

Now that she knew where the studio was, she turned to catch the bus back home, but a sign for a donut shop made her pause. It was a couple of hours since she'd had dinner, so she decided to drop in for a quick fill-up.

Having made her purchase, she carried the jelly donut and coffee to a corner table and settled down to do some people-watching. A donut shop was a great place for observing different characters, and Shaylee liked to imagine what the story behind each customer might be. A lonely old man sitting by himself. So sad. Two businesswomen with important-looking brochures between them, obviously having a meeting. A pretty blondie smiling at a handsome— Oh, God! It was Mike! Even from this distance she could see that smile to die for, complete with dimples.

Shaylee almost choked on her jelly donut. Was this a coincidence or what? She'd thought she would never see him again and here he was, big as life and twice as handsome. And a lovely blond woman sitting across the table from him. His girlfriend, no doubt about that, because judging from the way they were beaming at each other the lady definitely was *not* his sister.

Shaylee allowed herself a twinge of regret. Naturally a handsome hunk like that would have a girlfriend. Drat!

She finished the donut and gulped down the last of her coffee, but remained glued to her seat. She knew it was foolish to wait, but she didn't want to draw attention to herself by walking past them. Although, being so absorbed in each other, they probably wouldn't have noticed if she'd tap danced by them.

Finally, to her relief, the couple stood up and walked to the door, his arm possessively around her waist. She was laughing at something he'd said and his answering smile lit up his whole face. Shaylee wished she could see if the golden lights were dancing in his eyes, like at the gallery, but he was too far away.

After Mike and the blondie left, Shaylee got up and made her way out. What was Mike doing here, so close to the studio? Talk about donut shop mysteries. Well, the man had a girlfriend, no doubt about that. It wasn't as though she'd expected to one day fill that role. She'd only thought it would be nice to see him again. Which she had. So now her silly heart could slow down.

The excitement was over for the night.

A week later Shaylee opened the squeaking door number fifty-eight at street level and looked way up a long, narrow staircase leading to the second floor. Lugging her cumbersome art bag, she trudged up the stairs, taking in the peeling, dingy white paint on the walls.

Before she was halfway up she was puffing, and stopped for a breather. Had that good-looking Mike decided to take the classes? There was a tiny nibble of hope in her heart, because he'd said he probably should. And since seeing him in the donut shop a week ago, his brown eyes and dimples had persisted in invading her mind on more than one occasion. Like maybe a hundred occasions. The fact he had a girl-friend hadn't been a deterrent at all.

At the top of the stairwell Shaylee stood for a moment before a murky green door, where the missing paint chips revealed a layer of brown under navy blue. Maybe the art class should consider door-painting as one of its projects. Unless it was meant to give an artsy ambiance to the place.

A piece of paper taped to the door invited her to "Just walk in!" but Shaylee hesitated. Her heart hammered, and not just from the climb, because this was it. The moment of truth had arrived. Michael Merrick would soon tell her if her art was any good. Her hand clutched the worn brass doorknob as she fought back the old doubts that pushed their way to the surface.

Hopefully this Mr. Merrick wouldn't be as rigid and uncompromising as Mr. Crawley in high school had been.

"Miss Palmer," The old art teacher's stern voice still rang in her ears. "At this primary stage in one's art education one does not deviate from the rules. Learning about the colour wheel is an important first step, even if *you* seem to consider it somehow irrelevant and beneath you. Like in music, one does not jump into composing symphonies before one has first learned the scales."

"But what if one is Mozart?" Shaylee had countered impishly, to hide her fear.

"Miss Palmer," Mr. Crawley had snapped. "Are you implying *you* are as talented an artist as Mozart was a musician?" With his bushy gray eyebrows raised critically, he'd looked down his long nose at her, making her feel like a blob of spilled paint. "Please follow the instructions."

Even though she'd asked for it, this putdown in front of the entire class hadn't exactly reinforced her self-confidence.

Mr. Crawley, begone. Shaylee took a deep breath, exhaled, and entered the studio with what she hoped looked like a poised and purposeful step.

A few people had already arrived and were arranging their art materials on long folding tables lining the walls of the large, sterile room. No one seemed to notice her poised and purposeful entry, but through the wide, uncovered corner windows the flickering neon light from across the street winked its "WELCOME" sign at her.

She stood at the door for a moment. An elderly woman was setting out her paint equipment on a table in the far corner and didn't turn to look at her. Three men were chatting at the back of the room and Shaylee wondered which of them could be Mr. Merrick.

She removed her wool beret and was tugging at a mitten, when the tallest of the men turned. Seeing her, he grinned in recognition.

"Mike!" she cried in surprise and smiled with delight as he strode toward her with a long, easy step. "So you decided to take lessons after all." His faded jeans and white t-shirt were both multi-coloured from splattered paint in true artist fashion. So he *did* paint, at least on his clothes.

Mike held out his hand. "Hi. You must be Shaylee Palmer."

How did he know her name? The thought flashed through her mind, just as his next words dropped on her like a bombshell.

"I'm Michael Merrick."

Shaylee stared at the man, her forehead scrunched in confusion. "B-but I thought . . ." *Her* Mike was really Michael Merrick? Mike—Michael. Duh, of course. She could feel a flush of anger heat her cheeks. He should've introduced himself at the studio, instead of playing games with her, letting her prattle on and on about his work. Amusing himself at her expense.

Her annoyance must have been obvious to Michael, for he grimaced. "I know. I'm sorry. I was *going* to tell you, but then Max came in, and you left, and—" He spread his hands apologetically. "I've felt rotten all this time for having left you with the wrong impression. I shouldn't have continued the charade as long as I did, but you can imagine how flattered I was, listening to your candid praise of my work. You must forgive me."

"Sure," Shaylee decided to shrug off the incident. What would it serve to make a fuss and get into a tiff with her teacher on her first night? He hadn't lied about anything, after all, only neglected to set her straight on his identity. "Good thing I didn't ridicule your work, or I'd really feel uncomfortable right now."

"I don't know when I've received such warm and sincere praise. So could we maybe start again? Hi, I'm Michael Merrick."

Suddenly she realized the man was still holding out his hand in an unacknowledged greeting. With a short laugh, Shaylee started to fumble with her beret and mittens that she still gripped in her hands.

"Hi, I'm Shaylee Palmer." In her hurry to remove a mitten, she dropped her hat to the floor and bent to retrieve it.

Apparently Michael had the same idea, for as she crouched, so did he. Their heads collided with a resounding thump.

"I'm sorry," Michael said, straightening up. Wa-ay up, Shaylee observed from near the floor, where she still crouched, groping for the unfortunate beret. Her head was reeling, but she wasn't sure if it was because of the blow, or from looking into warm brown eyes, where those incredible golden lights were doing a dizzy dance. Or was it the bare light bulb, dangling on a cord directly above them, doing the dancing?

Michael held out his hand to help her. "Are *you* all right? You look a bit dazed. Here, come and sit down."

As Shaylee surrendered her hand to him, tingles tickled her fingertips. Wrapping his other arm around her shoulders, he walked her to the nearest folding chair.

Her head throbbed. Or was that her pulse doing a bouncy number? "I . . . I'm fine. Really I am. Are you okay?"

"No problem." He tapped his forehead and again that dimpled, boyish grin appeared. "Takes more than that to hurt this noggin."

And those eyes. Shaylee looked away. Sheesh. Was she developing an eye-fetish or something? Never had one before.

Michael held her hand even after she was safely seated. Shaylee marveled how nicely they fit together. She couldn't help taking a quick peek at his ring finger. Nope. No ring. Of course that didn't mean anything these days, but knowing Michael was *possibly* unattached gave her a small—albeit totally unreasonable—twinge of pleasure. Even though the face of the beautiful blondie in the donut shop was still firmly in her memory.

Ah, yes, the blondie. Quickly Shaylee pulled her hand away. Looking up, she caught something like disappointment flash across his face. As though she'd taken his candy away from him.

"You have a very unusual name," he mused. "I hope you don't mind, but I looked it up on the internet because I found it so intriguing. 'Fairy Princess of the Field'. Right?"

She glanced up, surprised. "I'm surprised you thought it could actually be a real name. Usually people assume it's a nickname, or something made up." She brought up a hand in teasing defense. "But please don't hold it against me. My grandpa was a sucker for fairy tales. He named me."

With a teasing grin he blurted out, "I can hardly wait to see the gauzy wings and transparent gowns a Fairy Princess hides under a heavy coat."

Obviously he meant that as a joke but she didn't want him to think she condoned such off-colour comments. Rising silently, she went to hang up her coat and then turned to face him.

"No wings," she announced, spreading out her arms. "No transparent gowns either. Just an old t-shirt." She left him standing there, looking slightly abashed, and brushed past him to an empty table by the wall, on which she deposited her bag with a thud. She wanted to believe the man hadn't meant to be crude. He'd just mistakenly shoved his foot into his mouth, just like she was constantly doing. He was forgiven.

Out of her bag she carefully pulled a messy, much-used paint tray and a pristine block of watercolour paper. Giddy as a first grader with a brand new box of sparkly markers, she arranged her paint tubes and brushes on the table in front of her. At the sink in the opposite corner, she filled her water dishes and returned to her seat.

"Hi. Is someone sitting on this chair?"

Shaylee turned to see a slightly plump woman, about her height, perhaps fortyish, carrying a cloth bag bulging with angular objects.

Before she had a chance to reply, the woman continued, "One of those mindless questions people always ask. Of course no one's sitting on this chair. So may I?"

Shaylee laughed. "Please do." She already liked this woman.

The newcomer plunked her bag on the table. A few dark strands of hair were trying to escape from under her beret, which competed with her lipstick for being the brightest red in the room.

"My name's Marita Osborne," she said, equally brightly and then added, out of one corner of her mouth, "I don't think I'm qualified for this class. Don't tell the teacher, but I lied on my application and said I'd done some painting in the past. Actually I'm a total neophyte."

She pulled a bunch of new-looking brushes from the bag and laid them on the table. "Well, it's not *exactly* a lie," she went on, "because we did art in grade school. This class is not too far from where I live, and by a strange coincidence it happens to be on the one night where I have an appalling blank on my social calendar." Marita finally drew a breath. "How about you?"

Shaylee was almost breathless at this outpouring of information. "I'm Shaylee Palmer and I've painted all my life," she revealed in turn. "But I've never actually taken proper lessons, so I thought I'd try this course and see where I've been messing up. I'm looking forward to learning from a real professional. Actually," she gave a short laugh that hid the seriousness behind her words, "what I'm really hoping he'll do is tell me I'm the greatest painter since Leonardo da Vinci." The words didn't come out sounding quite as jocular as she's hoped. Maybe because they were the truth.

Marita nodded and observed their teacher. "He does look like a real professional, doesn't he? Even his clothes are painted."

"Have you seen his work?" Shaylee licked the point of her thin rigger brush to make it sharp. "I fell in love with them at first sight."

"In love with him, did you say?"

"In love with them. His paintings," Shaylee corrected, emphatically. "Not him." Though she could see where that wouldn't be a huge stretch.

"Very good looking, our teacher," Marita murmured, as though reading her thoughts. "I wouldn't have been surprised if you'd said 'him'."

"I didn't."

"Okay." Marita hummed as she inspected the tubes of paint and read the labels. "It must have been some lover who dreamed up these names for paints. Listen to this one. Burnt Umber. Umber. Shadow. Dark. Hot. Sultry," she intoned.

Shaylee grinned. "It says all that on your tube? Mine only says Burnt Umber."

"Here's another one. Raw Sienna. R-r-raw, earthy." Marita wiggled her penciled eyebrows suggestively. "Sexy. Whew! A person could get hot just reading paint tube labels."

Shaylee's shoulders shook with giggles as she picked up another tube. "How about this one. Brown Madder."

"Yuck! Sounds like something you'd find at the bottom of a slop pail."

Shaylee's laughter rang out over the quiet buzz of conversation and although the people were busy setting up, most heads turned her way. Michael grinned at her from across the room and quirked an eyebrow, as if to ask what this hysteria was about.

"Now I'll never be able to paint with a straight face," Shaylee moaned, wiping her eyes. "If he says, 'Squeeze out some Brown Madder, please,' I might start to howl."

"And he would think you've flipped," Marita said over her shoulder as she walked to the sink. She returned, gingerly carrying a plastic margarine tub, filled to the brim with water. "Would the water dish be better on the left or on the right, do you think?"

"I think our teacher will set you straight on that," Shaylee replied absently. She was intent on observing

Michael, who was warmly welcoming a beautiful red-head at the door. With a kiss. On the mouth.

Shaylee stared in confusion. This wasn't the blondie from the donut shop, who, she'd assumed, was his girlfriend. Shouldn't this kind of a greeting be reserved for her?

Chapter Two

"Welcome back, Helena, sweetheart," Michael was saying to the woman. "I've missed you all summer."

Was his hand resting a tad too long on the woman's shoulder? Was his voice too teasing? Was his smile rather rakish? It seemed to Shaylee he was giving the woman the impression he'd been waiting for her since last spring.

What was going on?

The woman crossed to a table and began to take out her materials. As Michael went back to his table, at that moment, with a great flourish, the blondie from the donut shop entered.

"Hi, Britney," Michael called to her. "Prompt as usual."

The blondie beamed at him. "You know I'm always on time for your classes, Michael." She sashayed across the room and gave him a resounding kiss. On the mouth.

So the donut shop blondie was one of the students. But was she also his girlfriend? Or was Helena-sweetheart the girlfriend?

Shaylee looked on, more and more puzzled, as a tall, willowy woman entered and also received a kiss from the teacher.

"Hi, Sue. Haven't seen you in two weeks."

The woman laughed in response. "And you're still as good-looking as ever."

Shaylee shook her head. Not the way *her* teachers in high school had ever greeted her. Thank goodness. But this was the Big City and maybe things were done differently here. So he and this Sue had met two weeks ago, but there were no classes then.

A pair of very giggly ladies now entered, reminding Shaylee of an older version of a couple of giddy high school classmates. Michael greeted them each with a peck on the cheek and they responded with—what else?—giggles.

The scenario was beginning to amuse her. As she'd been growing up on the farm, she'd seen a lot of similar giggly goings-on between her seven handsome brothers and the neighbourhood maidens. So maybe things here weren't so different after all.

"My, isn't he a friendly puppy," Marita muttered. She'd obviously also been following the show.

"Well, I guess he likes to make everyone feel welcome," Shaylee said, but a sense of disappointment nibbled at her. The whole scenario seemed too frivolous. It looked like her Michael Merrick was some kind of a ladies' man. Pity. Reluctantly she downgraded his wonderful-index by a notch. Although, to be fair, a man with his good looks was bound to be a chick-magnet. And what man wouldn't relish so much female attention? She only hoped the art classes wouldn't turn out to be some kind of a Monday night love-in, because she fully intended to work hard and show him what she was capable of doing. In fact, she wanted to totally bowl him over in the process. Amaze and astound him, even.

By the time the class started there were ten students in the room and only two of them were men. A
timid looking pair, who stuck close to each other for
security among the females. She'd heard Michael refer
to them as Bruce and Burt. Or was it Burt and Bruce?

It soon became obvious that, with the exception of
Shaylee and Marita, all were returning students.
Shaylee hoped that was an indication of Michael's
teaching ability and not a testament of his popularity
with the ladies.

As if on cue, Britney's loud laughter drew Shaylee's
attention. The woman's hand rested on Michael's arm
possessively.

"Oh, Michael, you made the evening, as always," she
cooed. "You must come again this Friday." She looked
at him with a coquettish smile.

"Looks like he also gives private lessons," Marita
murmured, rolling her eyes.

Shaylee turned to face her. "Not nice," she mouthed
and tried to shrug off the growing sense of disappointment. What business was it of hers what lessons
Michael gave and to whom? It didn't mean he wasn't a
good art teacher. And he certainly was a wonderful
painter. Yet she couldn't help wondering how a man
who seemed to be such a frivolous lady-killer, could
produce paintings that exuded such depth of feeling.
The work she'd seen at the gallery had to mean something.

"I always welcome a home-cooked meal," Michael
was saying to Britney. "Especially when you're the
cook."

"And she cooks, too," Shaylee whispered with a sardonic grimace.

"Not nice," Marita mouthed, in turn.

Michael walked to their table and placed an arm around both their shoulders. "Hey, everyone," he announced. "I'd like you to meet your two new classmates, Shaylee Palmer and Marita Osborne."

Shaylee stiffened. She knew it was meant to be a friendly gesture but she resented his assumption that she would naturally welcome his touchy-feely familiarity. He must have sensed her discomfort, for he removed his arm and took a step back.

But strangely, his touch remained on her shoulder even after the hand had left. That puzzled her, and she only half-listened to his introductions. The giggly pair turned out to be Pauline and Tracy and the middle-aged lady in the corner was Peggy, who seemed to be the only hold-out to Michael's charms.

Shaylee was jolted out of her musings when she heard Britney say, "So *you're* the cupcake whose name so enthralled our teacher."

The woman's hooded eyes swept over Shaylee, taking in every detail, and made it very clear she didn't like cupcakes.

Shaylee kept her face blank, but the idea of her name being discussed and laughed at behind her back irked her. She heard Marita's quick intake of breath, indicating this new friend was ready to do battle on her behalf.

Michael scowled at Britney. "You know I only mentioned it the other night because it's so unusual." He gave Shaylee a lopsided grin. "I'm sorry. I didn't mean to be disrespectful or indiscreet."

Shaylee couldn't help the irritation that filled her. The man was committing one faux pas after another. Even more than *she* could manage on a good night.

First not coming clean with her at the gallery, then all the intimations about the Fairy Princess stuff, and now admitting he'd made her name the topic of conversation. And probably laughing about it.

"Michael's the very best teacher I've ever had," Britney announced, as if the previous exchange had never occurred. She gave her "very best teacher" an adoring smile and slid her hand lightly along his arm.

Michael's dismissive shrug didn't quite manage to hide his pleasure at the compliment.

Enough of this sideshow. Shaylee turned to her painting materials. It was time to get on with the lesson already.

As though reading her thoughts Michael asked everyone to come and watch a demonstration on how to lay a background wash and drop a line of trees on the horizon.

Soon the old pros went off to prepare a bluish-gray wash for an overcast winter sky while Michael came to chat with Shaylee and Marita. He explained about the weight and texture of the paper and why these were important considerations. He also talked about the brushes, explaining the purpose of each of the many shapes and sizes.

As Michael talked, Shaylee soaked in every bit of information. She found his words reassuring, for she'd been using these materials all along. Come to think of it, this was exactly what old Crawley had taught her.

"And you should have two containers for water," Michael concluded. "One for rinsing your brushes, and the other for adding clean water to paints, and for wetting the paper."

"Two?" Marita groaned. "I can't even figure out where to put *one*."

As he sat down to demonstrate a point for them, Shaylee watched how his hand moved the brush deftly on the paper. Large and strong, but also long-fingered and sensitive. She remembered how it had felt when it had held hers and she had a crazy impulse to slip her hand into his again in order to feel the delicious tingle that had tickled her fingers at his touch.

She tried to concentrate on his words, but his nearness disturbed her, making her conscious of how his tawny, straight hair fell over his forehead and covered the back of his neck down to the collar of his t-shirt. She wondered how the strands of hair would feel, slipping through her splayed fingers. Silky and smooth . .
.

She gave a start. Michael had asked a question. Something about the colour spreading evenly when a wash was applied to wet paper.

"Yes, I see," she responded automatically, hoping it was the correct answer.

"See how it gives a soft background for the winter scene?" Michael went on and turned to look at Shaylee, who nodded and kept her eyes on the painting. No way was she going to look at him.

This man was totally distracting her. Making her all confused. His smile with those nice dimples. Nice? The dimples were *sexy*. And he probably knew it, too, and used them for his own—

Shaylee stopped the thought in mid-think. What Michael Merrick did with his dimples, or with any other part of his anatomy, was absolutely no business of hers. She steered her mind back to the lesson, but with his back turned toward her, she couldn't help stealing peeks at the dorsal muscles that rippled under the soft fabric of his t-shirt.

He probably looked terrific on a beach without a shirt. With seven brothers, it wasn't as though she had never seen a man's bare back, or more. She was totally accustomed to seeing males in various stages of undress, but couldn't help admiring Michael's anatomy. No wonder the women all seemed to be so enamored of their teacher. And at this rate, if she didn't watch herself, she would soon be joining the ranks of these groupies.

"Okay, ladies. You're on your own."

Michael's voice brought Shaylee back from the beach. He set them to work to lay a wash on their paper and advised them to keep their brushes full and their strokes even. Then he went off to check on the others. The giggly pair, Pauline and Tracy, immediately commandeered his attention with their whiny requests.

"Oh, Michael," one of them squealed. "My sky is turning out too streaky. What am I doing wrong?"

Marita soon echoed this question, as her paper took on a similar striped appearance. "What's happening?" she wailed to Shaylee. "It looked so easy when he did it."

But Shaylee painted on, now totally absorbed in her work. The brush felt like a natural extension of her hand, went exactly where she'd planned, swirled just the way she wanted. It was almost magical. Her self-confidence soared. Surely Michael couldn't help noticing how easily she accomplished these excellent results. The grasses were almost growing off the paper.

"Not bad." Michael had approached quietly on his rounds and now stood behind her chair. As he leaned forward, his thigh brushed lightly against her, causing her hand to jerk in response. A long blade of grass shot off to one side.

"Oh, drat!" she exclaimed.

"That's okay," Michael reassured her. "Grasses are supposed to go every which way."

Shaylee exhaled in exasperation. "But that's not the direction *I* was going to have it go." She turned to look up at him as she spoke.

His eyebrow rose, along with the corners of his mouth. "Control freak, are we?"

"Well, I like to be the boss of my own grasses," she riposted, trying to keep her words light, despite the disturbing effect his nearness was having on her. She turned back to her painting, but the hairs on the nape of her neck still strongly signaled his presence.

Michael moved on, while Shaylee began to rub out the wayward reed with a stiff scrub brush. But in her agitation she succeeded in almost breaking the surface of the paper, while a watermark suddenly formed on the gray sky. Desperately she tried to sponge it out with a bit of tissue, but managed to botch up the picture even more.

Heaving a huge, impatient sigh, she raked her fingers through her curls. So much for showing him how good she was. As she rinsed out her brush, her disobedient eyes roamed afield, fixating on the rough features of Michael's bare, muscular arm, as he leaned his hand on the nearby table. The thought of that arm around her shoulders only a few heartbeats ago produced an involuntary shiver of delight.

No wonder she was messing up, concentrating on the teacher instead of her work. She banged the brush on the bottom of the water container.

Michael turned to look. "That ought to get the pigment out," he commented with a grin.

Britney's high-pitched laughter rang out over friendly chuckles. Shaylee decided not to throw her brush at the woman. The dirty water, maybe, but not her expensive brush.

With Michael away from her, giving assistance to the others, Shaylee tried to direct her attention back to her work. But the simple winter scene on her paper definitely was not taking on the delicate appearance she'd been striving for when she began the painting with such great optimism. The rubbed-out blob glared like a garish reminder of her distracted state of mind, and she could swear the disgusting watermark smirked at her.

Annoyed with herself, she ripped the sheet off the pad with an angry, overblown gesture. In the quiet room the sound immediately drew everyone's attention to her. Marita tsk-tsked softly beside her, but wisely made no comment. Shaylee did her best not to blush. Instead she shrugged, crumpled the paper and casually aimed it at the wastebasket. Of course she missed and had to walk to the center of the room to retrieve the ball, conscious of every eye following her actions.

"I thought I'd begin again," she muttered to no one in particular as she walked back to her table. "That one was beyond fixing."

Michael glanced at the round, utilitarian clock on the back wall. "Okay. But you don't have much time."

It didn't take her long to lay a new background wash and paint on the trees. She blew the paper dry with a hair blower and began to add in the details, determined not to mess up again. This time the trees and the dry grasses peeking through the snow had an aura of peaceful, wintry silence, just as she'd envisioned.

As she painted, quickly and deftly, Shaylee had the

disturbing feeling that someone was watching her. And sure enough, when she raised her eyes, they met Michael's from across the room.

He walked to her table, picked up her paint board, and scrutinized the work. She cringed inwardly. Old Mr. Crawley once again loomed over her.

"I've always loved watercolours," she said tentatively, trying to ward off her feeling of insecurity.

"That's good." Michael put the painting down and moved on.

Was that a comment on her work, or the fact she liked watercolours? Shaylee muttered a quiet "Thank you," and tried to smile pleasantly at his receding back.

Although her second attempt was a hurried one, she found the end product quite pleasing. When the class was over, everyone walked around the room to see what had been produced. Shaylee's painting received effusive praises, and even Britney's muffled comment sounded very much like, "Pretty good".

But what would the teacher say?

Michael's reaction stymied her. "Okay," he said, glancing briefly at the painting.

But before Shaylee had a chance to analyze his laconic observation, Marita broke in eagerly. "And mine? How's my first attempt at painting since kindergarten?"

With a studied, serious expression, Michael bent to examine the work, his head pensively cocked to one side. "Hmmm. You've probably made some progress since then."

Marita's easy laughter rang out. "Now, that's a diplomatic answer if I ever heard one."

When they'd packed up and were preparing to leave,

Michael came to the door, where Shaylee was buttoning up her coat.

"So, where did you take lessons?" he asked abruptly.

Shaylee was taken aback, but replied saucily, "Well, I took a few lessons from Leonardo da Vinci, but we didn't do too much with watercolours. Mainly oils and sculptures, you know." Was that why he'd been looking at her during the class? Had he thought she'd lied on her application when she said she hadn't taken art lessons previously? Of course his question could have had a positive significance, like maybe he thought her work was good.

"You've painted a lot though." Michael stated.

"I've only done stuff on my own," she mumbled, embarrassed by his disregard of her feeble attempt at comedy. Then, hoping to show him she wasn't a total neophyte, she continued brightly, "I love the luminous quality of watercolours and—"

"I'm sure you'll make fine progress."

His words sounded dismissive and disappointment stabbed at her heart. "Thank you," she said quietly.

This first lesson certainly hadn't proved to be the confidence-booster she'd hoped for. Silly girl, expecting him to be impressed by her first attempt. Chewing on her bottom lip, Shaylee turned to go.

But now the grin she'd earlier found so disarming, appeared on his face. "Good night. See you next week."

And suddenly the room became overheated and Shaylee felt a warm flush creep up to her cheeks. Had to be the bulky scarf.

"Good night," she blurted and hurried down the narrow stairwell, catching up to Marita outside on the sidewalk.

They both walked to the same bus stop.

"So, where do you live?" Marita asked. "I'm waiting for number 96, myself."

"Me too," Shaylee said. "I live at the old Windsor Arms walk-up a few kilometres down the street. I've been there just three months."

"You're kidding! That's my building, too. Fourth floor."

"Ah, the penthouse. I'm on the third. Funny I haven't run into you before."

Marita gave Shaylee a friendly pat on the shoulder. "Welcome to the 'hood."

A near-empty bus drove up and they climbed on. As soon as they were settled in their seats, Marita brought up the very subject Shaylee had decided she would not think about.

"I fear our teacher's brown eyes and that gorgeous grin are going to turn even my old knees into mush." Marita rolled her round, dark eyes. "When he greeted me at the door, I tell you, he made me feel as though I was fifteen years younger and twenty pounds lighter."

Shaylee laughed. "Yes, I guess his charms are going to be pretty difficult to resist." Hadn't she already begun to fall under their spell tonight? And messed up her painting in the process.

"Amen. I hear you, sister," Marita breathed. "But isn't it going to be delicious, feasting our eyes on him every Monday night? I noted the other gals in the room were doing just that. And my guess is, our teacher doesn't mind one bit being the object of all that adoration." She chuckled and pulled the bell rope. "The shameless Lothario."

"So where's Laine gallivanting right now? Still some-where on the Dark Continent?" Max Storm reached for the brown manila envelope Michael held out to him.

"Still there. You'll love these sketches he sent. I never get postcards from him, just art."

"*Just* art?" Max pulled a paper with a pencil sketch from the envelope. "This is great. A mother with an in-fant at her breast. Beautiful. That partner of yours sure knows how to pick his subjects. I'm looking for-ward to seeing the finished canvas on the wall of my gallery." He drew out more papers and his eager brown eyes gloated over each sketch.

Michael grimaced and shook his head as he ob-served the proprietor's greedy face. "Yeah, you'll get a lot of great art from him to sell here, Max."

"As opposed to what I'm getting from you, now." Being somewhat shorter, Max had to bend his head back to show Michael his disappointed expression.

When Michael didn't reply, Max put the sketches on a low table, beside some brochures. "So, when *can* I expect more work from you?" He waved his hand around the room. "I like to change the displays now and then, you know."

"Yeah, I know, I know." Michael took in the paint-ings on the walls with an inward grimace. "I've been busy with commissioned work." He couldn't very well reveal to Max he had no more work to give. At least not good enough to be exhibited. And the frustrating thing was, he couldn't even explain to himself what the prob-lem was.

"Yes, we all have to eat and pay our bills, but you and I both know it's your creative work that defines you. You poured your heart and soul into these paint-ings and it shows. That's the reason they're in my gallery, I might add." Max paused. "So, what *are* you doing these days?"

"Designing a huge mural for a bank lobby in Montréal, for one thing. I already told you, I don't have time for this stuff right at the moment. I'll get back to it when Mika returns from Africa and I get some slack."

Max cast a sharp look at Michael. "*Stuff?* You're calling this *stuff?* You've always made time for this *stuff* before, no matter how busy you were. Your painting *always* came first. And I'm not talking about painting murals. They may be an art form, too, but not something *I* can hang on *my* walls and sell."

Michael raised his hands in defense. "Hey, don't get your knickers in a knot. I'll get back to it."

"When?"

"I already told you. When Mika gets back and takes over some of the more mundane work."

"And then it'll be your turn to take off for Europe, or wherever you're going next summer. Goodbye."

"That's still months away," Michael snapped. "I'll produce something before that." Then, seeing the skeptical look on Max's face, he exhaled in frustration. He hated to be evasive with his old friend but, dammit, better to pretend he didn't have the time, than to admit the truth. He just couldn't paint any more.

"I know you wouldn't go to another gallery behind my back, or anything."

The proprietor's silky smooth voice made Michael's temper flare up. "I hope that's an affirmation and not a question."

At that the other man's face turned slightly ruddier than it already was.

Michael's brows drew together darkly. At least Max had the courtesy to blush after a comment like that, dammit!

"Michael, we've been doing business for several years, and we've always been up-front with each other. Right? Never a problem. Right?"

"That's right." Never a problem till this present one. And he wasn't going to explain it to Max, because this—whatever was causing it—would pass in due time. Just a normal, garden-variety dry spell. A painter's block, so to speak.

Max nodded and then, to Michael's relief, he turned his piercing eyes away from him, to point at a winter scene on the wall.

"This one's my favourite," Max said. "I'd love to buy it for myself, but I hate to lose the commission on it."

Michael laughed. "Max, my friend, you're such a sentimental fool."

"Come on, Michael," Max scoffed. "You know perfectly well I'm generous to a fault, in some ways."

Michael chuckled. "Yeah, as long as it doesn't have to do with money." He knew Max wasn't offended by the ribbing.

"Hey, gimme a break. Don't I always give a leg up to a promising artist when I meet one?"

Michael's face turned serious. "Yes, you're right. Me, for instance."

"Well, you had your parents to push you up the ladder and—" Max began, but stopped cold.

Anger flashed through Michael's brain. "Are you saying my paintings aren't good enough on their own? That without my parents' influence, they wouldn't be here?"

"Michael, Michael." Max waved a placating hand, causing several diamond rings to glitter under the spotlights. "Of course I'm not saying that. You know your paintings are fabulous. The rave reviews your work has received should assure you of that. Don't be so quick to jump out of your thin skin, for God's sake! You artists," he snorted. "I don't know why I put up with you."

Michael kept his gaze glued to his feet, feeling foolish about his childish outburst. "So what were you implying then?"

"I wasn't implying anything. I only wanted to point out it was your parents' involvement with the arts that brought your work to my attention in the first place. I'm sure I would've heard of you eventually, but it might have taken a bit longer if the Merricks hadn't sent their super-talented young son to my gallery with a painting under his arm."

"I don't know if he's so super-talented any more," Michael muttered, almost to himself. There, he'd said it. Picking up the manila envelope, he pushed the brochures off to one side and slumped down to sit on the low table. He leaned his elbows on his knees, feeling about as super-talented as the dead fly on the carpet by his foot.

"Hey, listen," Max squeaked, and dug his fingers into Michael's shoulder. "You'll get over it. Everyone does."

"I wonder."

"Sometimes a divorce takes this long to get over," Max said. "Not that I can relate to that. Delight is what I felt when *my* marriage ended. And believe me, one of these mornings you'll wake up and ask yourself, 'Ashley who?'."

Divorce? His divorce had nothing to do with it. During his short, tumultuous marriage Michael had quickly become aware that Ashley's love for him didn't

encompass his art. But he and his art were insepara-
ble, an artist's version of "Love me, love my dog". Ashley's demands, which he'd considered selfish, had
made him cynical about women, and during the few
years the marriage had lasted this belief had gained a
deep foothold in his mind. Who needed a wife? Art was
his wife and his only love. Sex he could always get on
the side.

Although now it seemed that even this love had deserted him. His ability to view the world with bright,
positive enthusiasm had evaporated. The paintings he
produced these days just didn't give him that feeling
of pure joy and satisfaction his previous works had
done. Something was gone. It was as though he had
nothing inside to give.

How the hell could nothing fill a person so completely?

When Michael didn't respond for a time, Max went
on. "Let me tell you, as a friend, it's natural to have a
dry spell after a divorce. But let me also tell you," his
voice no longer had the congenial, chummy tone, "that
as a gallery owner, I wish to God you'd snap out of it.
Soon. It's not good for my business to display the work
of an artist who's—"

Michael stiffened and his head jerked up. "Who's
what? Washed up?"

"*Dried* up, is what I was going to say. But if you
don't start producing something soon . . ."

"I haven't dried up!" Michael wanted to shout, but
he kept his mouth shut. Because he had. He painted
and painted but what he produced was crap. The
paintings weren't alive, not like the ones on these
walls. And for sure he wasn't going to bring that
garbage for Max to see, because he knew they would

get a disappointing reception. And deservedly so.

It was too painful to look around at his past work. "I'll produce," he said, glaring at the dead fly on the rug. "Don't you worry." Yeah, he could do the worrying very nicely all on his own, thanks.

Then, to get the spotlight off himself, Michael stood up and stretched.

"By the way, I have a new student," he said, forcing his voice to sound casually conversational. "In fact, you actually saw her a while ago here at the gallery. Remember? I was chatting with her when you came in." He knew Max could recall every pretty woman who had ever walked through the doors of his gallery.

Max nodded. "The cute little one? With the big boots and long dark overcoat?"

"That's the one. And after observing her in the first class, I'd say she's very good."

"Very good?" Interest flashed in Max's beady brown eyes.

"I think so. I'm already getting excited about guiding her along. She'll be a fine painter."

"So, if she's that good, why's she with you? Your classes are for beginners and for casual hobbyists, aren't they? With 'follow-the-leader' kind of lessons?"

Michael grinned. "Yeah. I guess that's one way of putting it. I do a demonstration lesson on some technique and they try to paint something using it. The operative word here is 'try'. They all have some flair for art, but not one of them is exactly Michelangelo. And I'm sure they don't do any painting outside the classes."

The image of Shaylee flashed into Michael's brain again, as it had countless times since Monday night. Those huge, violet eyes, fringed with long lashes hadn't left him in peace. It was as though this Fairy of the Field, this little sprite bundled up in a heavy winter coat and boots, had woven some incredible spell over him.

When he'd held her delicate hand in his, he couldn't believe how well it fit there. He glanced furtively at her other hand for a ring. No ring. He couldn't think of a logical reason for the relief that had washed through him, except that no man had the right to put a claim on a free-flying sprite. Too bad he'd made that goofy comment about gauzy wings and transparent gowns because that almost got them off to a bad start. Luckily she'd not held it against him.

Michael grinned to himself. She was so petite, he'd felt like a six-foot giant, towering over her. And those short blond curls, framing her heart-shaped face. Adorable. No wonder her face had been constantly flashing into his mind in the two weeks before classes started. He'd found himself mentally crossing his fingers, hoping she would fill in the application form she'd picked up.

And she had.

Michael jerked out of his reverie when Max said, "So, you were saying she's very good?"

"Yes, she certainly is. And what I found especially fascinating was her delicate touch with the brush."

"So, I ask you again, what's she doing in your class, then?"

"I don't know," Michael mused. "Maybe she didn't read the brochure very carefully."

"So are you going to suggest she should enroll in a more advanced class?"

"Good point, Max." He'd been thinking about that, but had convinced himself that after just one class it *probably* was too early to tell if she was ready for more challenging work.

"Well?"

"First I want to see how good she actually is," Michael said evasively. "After one class you can't always tell. But I must admit I was damned surprised by what she produced. Surprised and impressed."

"Impressed? By a new student's work? Interesting."

"Yes. And you're right. I probably should advise her she's in the wrong class." Of course he should. But something in him didn't want to. If she left, he would never see her again. But of course that wasn't the reason.

"You know, Max, if she really turns out to be as good as I think she is, then I'm kind of reluctant to let someone else take over teaching her. I'd like to mentor her myself. Kind of like my parents did with young, talented artists." He grinned, slightly embarrassed. Did he sound a bit audacious? "Must be a family trait, this mentoring thing."

"Yes!" Max snapped his fingers under Michael's nose and a familiar gleam lit up the already bright eyes.

"Oh-oh. What?"

"No, listen, Michael," Max enthused. "Here's your chance to get into the act and help a young artist get started. She can be your very own protégée. Maybe you could even take her to Europe with you when you go next summer, show her the great galleries and churches and the whole art scene. How does that sound?"

Michael had to laugh. Despite his age, Max had a youthful habit of jumping in with both feet when a brilliant idea occurred to him. "Taking her to Europe seems a bit of a leap at this point, don't you think? I hardly know the woman."

"Seems to me you've never had a problem striking up relationships with ladies. I recall a beauty you took to dinner after barely having said hello to her here in my gallery. And whatever you two did afterward . . ." Max did the nudge-nudge, wink-wink with his eyes and one elbow. "Comparatively speaking, a two-hour art class is like an eternity, and more than enough time to make this young lady's acquaintance."

Michael frowned and his hand shot up as if to defend the reputation of his little Field Fairy. "Yeah, but she's not like that," he said firmly. He resented the implication that Shaylee would consent to such a thing. Though, what did he know about her? She could have had any number of lovers in her life. She seemed so innocent, but that didn't mean she was Virgin Mary. After all, she was a very pretty woman and it was hard to believe she didn't have a serious boyfriend.

"Okay. So maybe she won't jump into bed with you, but she could still be your masterpiece." Max's exuberance continued to bubble. "Kind of Pygmalion-like. You know, the whole 'My Fair Lady' thing. Maybe that would give you a reason to bounce out of bed in the morning."

"Hey, I don't need a reason to bounce out of bed," Michael riposted. But yes, he did. His art sure didn't inspire him to jump to his atelier. Not like it used to.

"You know what I mean," Max insisted. "It might be an inspiration for you to have someone to mentor."

"Pygmalion-like? That's really stretching it. And I don't even know if she's as good as all that. I mean, we've only had one class, for Pete's sake."

But for a second the idea *did* sound feasible, even

exciting. If she was talented, maybe he *could* help her develop and then bring her to the attention of the art world. Then his enthusiasm faded and he frowned. "What you're saying is, since I can't create art myself, maybe I can create *her* into something, eh? Is that what you're getting at? 'Them that can, do. Them that can't, teach.' Max, your faith in me is touching."

Max slapped his shiny forehead in frustration. "There you go again, putting words in my mouth. What I tried to say is, by helping this girl you could help yourself."

Yeah, another foolish, bellicose reaction. He knew exactly what Max was getting at. "I know, I know. I'm sorry." These days he was too quick to take offense at anything that even faintly hinted at his problem. And no wonder. If the proprietor could only see the piles of ruined art in his atelier . . .

His attempt at a grin almost failed. "Maybe one day I'll bring *her* creations to you, if not my own. Then you'll have something to sell. It's the least I can do for a friend."

Max heaved a huge, exasperated sigh and threw up his arms. "Michael, why don't you do me a great big favour? Go jump off a bridge!"

"Maybe I will." Michael followed him out of the room. "But first I want a cup of coffee. Got any in your office?"

Chapter Three

"Ow! Blast it!"

Shaylee's thumb flew into her mouth, the hammer dropped on her big toe, and the picture hook and nail fell with tiny clinks onto the parquet floor. Hopping around the living room, she clutched her smarting toe, while sucking on the throbbing thumb. When the pain in both had subsided, she retrieved the hook, nail, and hammer from the floor, and resumed her hammering—very gingerly this time.

By her feet a large watercolour painting leaned against the wall. She lifted it up and carefully hung it on the hook. The gilded frames picked up the glow from the lamp on the side table. She stepped back a few feet, seated herself cross-legged on the floor, and then sat there, head tilted to one side, losing herself in the peaceful harmony of the scene.

A road, leading . . . where? Trees, their leaves softly touched by the balmy evening breeze. The golden fields of waving grasses, dotted here and there with the subdued colours of wildflowers. A shimmering lake in the distance bathed in the luminescent afterglow of a beautiful day.

"Well, *I* like it. I don't care about anyone else." Shaylee spoke the words aloud, nodding defiantly, but she knew she was only whistling in the dark. She *did* care. Very much. She'd poured her heart and soul into the painting, along with a huge amount of love for her country roots. And the thought of someone calling it just another "nice" painting by an amateur farm girl, caused a hard knot to form in her stomach, a pain worse than any hammer falling on her toe.

A few soft knocks on the door interrupted her contemplation. Who could that be, this late in the evening? Shaylee glanced at the painting, ran a quick hand through her curls and then, hammer in hand, went to the door. She squinted through the peephole and a smile replaced her frown.

"Open up, li'l sis," a cheerful male voice called.

Quickly Shaylee unlocked the door. "Ron! What're you doing in Toronto?"

A tall man in a bulky winter jacket stepped in, his large frame shrinking the small foyer. His straw-coloured hair was dusted with snow and he had the distinct look of a farmer, right down to his big, calloused hands, now reaching out for her.

"First let's have a proper greeting for the biggest and handsomest of your brothers," he growled and picked Shaylee up in his arms. "I haven't seen my one and only baby sister for three whole months." He twirled her around a few times and then deposited her on the floor with rough playfulness.

"Hey, take it easy." Shaylee held her head as she dizzily wobbled toward the kitchenette. "So, what *are* you doing in Toronto? Did Mum send you here to check up on me?"

The joke elicited a loud guffaw from Ron. "Yup. She

wanted me to check real discreet-like if you have any food in there." He nudged his head toward the fridge. "And I'm also supposed to report to her if you've gotten any thinner." He took a look at Shaylee's slim build and shook his head. "Nope. You're about as scrawny as before."

Shaylee puffed out her cheeks. "Next time I go home I'll walk in looking like a chipmunk. That'll make Mum happy." She got a milk container from the fridge and poured out two glasses. "And here are some chocolate chip cookies I baked yesterday. I must've suspected you were coming." She reached into a cookie jar and handed him a few.

Leading the way into the sparsely furnished living room, she set the glasses on the coffee table. The painting on the wall made her slightly uncomfortable. It was as conspicuous as a single cloud on a blue summer sky. But, just as she'd expected, Ron paid no mind to it and, without removing his jacket, heaved himself onto the sky-blue two-seater sofa. He picked up his milk glass and stuffed two cookies into his mouth.

Still, Shaylee couldn't help feeling miffed to have her work so cavalierly ignored.

"So, are you going to tell me what *really* brings you to the big city?" she asked again, swallowing down her irritation. "Or is it a secret? A woman, perhaps?"

Ron grinned and brushed aside her probing question with a dismissive wave. "Nope, no woman. I just came to pick up a part for the tractor, rather than wait two weeks for them to deliver it. But Mum made me promise to drop by and see how you're getting on." He shrugged. "I know I should've called first, but I figured you'd be home since it's this late. Hope you don't mind."

"Mind? You've no idea how happy I am to see your ugly old face." Shaylee sat beside Ron on the sofa and laid her head on his broad shoulder.

Ron's eyes narrowed with concern. "You sound like you're lonely here. Why don't you come back home? Mrs. Hallman can't seem to find anyone as good as you for fashioning those cute bridal bouquets 'n' stuff. And you know Mum and Dad would be happier than—"

"Pigs in a manure pile. Yes, I know. But it's taken me three months to get settled here in my cozy little apartment. I couldn't go back now. All this beautiful furniture I've scraped together. And these lovely antiques."

"I recollect you telling Mum you got them at the Salvation Army store," Ron reminded her.

"Not all of them. This sofa is a respectable second-hand item from a home sale." She bounced up and down a few times. "No squeaks, even. And all those little knick-knacks on Mum's doilies remind me of home. And guess what? I've finally mastered using the subway!"

"Way to go, Squirt."

Shaylee was proud of having made the difficult move away from her loving, but overprotective home. She didn't want to even debate returning, though her parents had tried earnestly on several occasions to change her mind.

"I'm not about to work in a flower shop for the rest of my life," Shaylee had retorted firmly to her parents, causing her mother to lament that her youngest child was spoiled and willful.

"You're so little and the city is so big," was her mother's favourite line.

"Mum, I'm not going to grow any bigger. I'm five foot two and that's exactly what I'll always be. Blame your inferior genes."

"Genes? My inferior genes didn't seem to affect your brothers' sizes any."

Even now Shaylee had to smile at the memory. Her mother always made it sound as though Shaylee had deliberately chosen to be the smallest of her eight kids.

Ron put an arm around her shoulder and gave her a squeeze. "But I gotta tell you, Mum's so impressed you got that assistant office manager's job at the insurance company. She's been bragging about it to everybody." He chuckled. "Assistant office manager. It sounds so important to her."

"Ron!" Shaylee bounced up from the sofa and her voice squealed in indignation. "It is important."

"Yeah, of course it is, Squirt," Ron protested also getting up. "I only meant—"

"Yes?" With fists planted defiantly on her hips, she dared him to tell her exactly what he thought.

But Ron deftly changed the subject and waved a big hand toward the opposite wall. "Hey, isn't that one of your paintings on the wall there? Kinda looks like the stuff you used to paint at home."

Stuff. "Yes, it is," she snapped.

"Nice job, Doodle-bug."

Shaylee knew he was trying to make up for his thoughtless comment about her job, and rewarded him with a toothy grimace. "A nice job, you say? Thank you, Ron. I'm surprised you recognize my style."

Ron grinned, obviously relieved he'd managed to pull that one out of the fire. "Hey, I'd recognize your doodles anywhere."

Shaylee sighed. She knew not to expect more laudatory words from a family member. Being called a Doo-dle-bug all her life hadn't exactly been a confidence-booster, but of course her family had never intended it as a put-down. She understood that. As a toddler, running from one brother to another, she'd demanded that everyone admire her "pitchurs".

"Look, Josh, lookit my pitchur."

"Very nice, Doodle-bug." Pat-pat on the head.

"Look, James, lookit my pitchur."

"Yeah, nice job, Short Stuff. I'm reading. You run along and play." A gentle whump on the bottom.

And off she'd scamper to the next brother.

Ron began to zip up his jacket, but Shaylee stopped him, placing a hand on his arm to indicate her forgive-ness.

"Speaking of painting, did Mum tell you I started art classes? I had my first class on Monday night." No way was she going to mention the handsome teacher. Nor was she going to tell Ron the handsome teacher hadn't said anything laudatory about her painting. Of course it had been just the first class, but still . . .

"That's great, Munchkin. A nice hobby. Keep you out of trouble here in the big city." Ron grinned, obvi-ously vying for her good graces.

Hobby. Shaylee forced herself to swallow her annoy-ance and said nothing.

"But your art teacher better be nicer to you than old Creepy Crawley at Runnymede High," Ron continued in his protective big brother voice.

"Oh, I'm sure he will be." If she played along the way Britney and the other women seemed to be doing, she was sure he would be *very* nice to her. "At the art class I met a woman who lives in this same building. She's a lot of fun. I think we're going to be good friends."

"That's great." Ron gave Shaylee a pat on the head. She cringed inwardly, but stayed put.

He dug his truck keys from his pocket. "Now you take care of yourself and have fun at your art classes."

Fun? If she wanted to, she could probably have *lots* of fun. The kind Ron could never imagine his baby sister indulging in. And he'd be right. She never would.

But Toronto was a big city and maybe one day she would meet a man with whom she could become friends, and eventually, maybe even something deeper. The way she'd been with Steve back home. He was a nice young man, and she still felt a twinge of regret for having had to tell him she was going away. They had been friends since the beginning of high school and as they'd grown closer, they had started to date. Together they'd learned the secrets of making love.

It had all been very beautiful, but Shaylee knew he was not the one she would spend the rest of her life with. He was, and always would be, a good friend, a solid farm boy, while she had her dreams of becoming a professional artist. She'd had to tell him about her goals, or how else could she have made him understand why she was leaving? And although they'd agreed to live their lives in complete freedom, she knew Steve was waiting for her. He called once in a while and always said he missed her.

"Could you say 'Hi' to Steve, when you see him?" she now asked Ron, to ease her guilt.

To her surprise, she had soon discovered she didn't miss Steve at all. Her parents, yes, the beautiful farm country, definitely, but the moments with Steve were blending in with all the other beautiful memories of her life back home.

After closing the door behind her brother, Shaylee

wandered back into the living room and stood, arms akimbo, in front of the painting.

"Yup. It's a nice job, all right," she mimicked, but then quickly sobered. What would her new art teacher say about it, *if* she ever got up the nerve to show this painting to him? Maybe he would tell her she wasn't nearly as talented as she imagined herself to be. And then what? Her ultimate and absolute dream of becoming a professional artist would be dashed. She had mapped out her life and made the move to Toronto with such optimism, yet she couldn't shake these pernicious doubts. She walked to the painting and gave the frame a few comforting strokes. Then she retreated to her bedroom, where she plumped up the pillows on her single bed.

"That stupid painting will never see the world beyond these walls," she muttered to herself. What had possessed her to spend so much of her hard-earned money getting it framed? Not to mention triple matted. With non-glare glass, even. Was that vanity or what?

She pulled off her navy-checkered flannel shirt and flung it on the floor. The jeans followed. In her blue wool socks, pink bra and panties she marched into the bathroom and squeezed toothpaste onto her toothbrush.

"Forget the doubts, Shaylee," she said aloud to her reflection and then began to brush vigorously. Art was her life and nothing and no one would be allowed to detract her from that goal. For the present, this was her own secret, but one day the whole world would know of her.

Ptooey! Down the drain went her doubts. *Ptooey*! Down went her family's put-downs. *Ptooey*! Down went

the disapproval of critical—*ptooey!*—old Creepy Crawley.

In the silent, empty studio Michael opened the wall
cupboard that housed the painting materials he used
for the class. He reached in for the things he would
need for tonight's lesson, and at the same time prepared himself to meet Shaylee again. For some reason
he'd been thinking about her all week. Like non-stop.
Day and night. And the weird thing was, he couldn't
figure out why he'd imagined that he'd seen censure
in those huge, violet eyes of hers last week. Ridiculous.
He must have read her wrong because what reason
could she possibly have for disapproving of him? After
all, she didn't even know him. So why the hell had she
made him feel like he should be booed off the stage?

Of course there had been no reason to mention this
particular fact to Max when they met on Thursday.
But why on earth did he have to go and spout off about
her so-called talent? What if last week's assignment
only happened to be something she did well? It was
just a simple winter scene. So she knew how to lay a
wash very nicely and paint a pretty good forest, not to
mention the dry, wispy grasses peeking through the
snow. And all those subtle shadows in just the right
places. Okay, so she could paint a damn convincing
winter scene, but so what? After one lesson, he could-
n't tell how good she really was. Some people could
draw fabulous horses, or maybe dogs, but ask them to
draw a tree, or a human, and they were totally at a
loss. He'd seen that so many times.

Michael walked around, placing milkweed pods on
the tables. He'd picked them up from a field on the
outskirts of the city.

But aside from her reproaching eyes, there were other things about this Shaylee-Fairy that also had stayed with him throughout the week. Like the way she held her head to one side as she listened to his instructions, seeming to suck in every word. Or the way her alert eyes observed his moves, and the way she nodded her understanding, as if confirming something to herself. All that would make any teacher feel appreciated. And the way she chewed on the end of her brush when deep in thought. Or the way she plowed her fingers through her curls when frustrated with her work. Or how her wide smile lit up the whole room when something amused her.

Or perhaps she'd been on his mind because—if he was honest with himself—she had succeeded in raising his hopes that maybe he'd finally found what every teacher dreams of. Not a dilettante out to fill a few empty hours on a Monday night, but a real student, eager to learn, with genuine, natural talent. Maybe she would even turn out to be a prodigy.

When he thought of her observations in the gallery about the "happy accident" with his winter scene, he had to shake his head in disbelief. Because that's exactly what had happened. He'd been trying to get the right effect of sunlight scintillating on the snow and had achieved it with a simple lucky brush stroke.

He set out a few tubes of paints they would be needing tonight, in case some students didn't own all the necessary pigments.

Obviously that was why he'd been so preoccupied with her. Because maybe, at last, he'd found his ideal student. Why hadn't he thought of that earlier, instead of concentrating on the unpleasant feeling of being rebuked by her lovely eyes?

Relieved at having found the cause for his seven-day itch, Michael whistled as he arranged the brushes for his demonstration lesson. But when Shaylee entered the studio with Marita, he couldn't help feeling apprehensive.

Shaylee kept her eyes averted from Michael as much as possible for fear he might mistake her eagerness to paint for something else. Like an eagerness to see him, for instance. Being used to his admiring groupies, he just might assume that. But with her, that *definitely* was not the case. She was there for the art and not to carry on a titillating Monday night intrigue. Period. She settled herself at the long table beside Marita, trying to strike an air of total control and confidence.

Throughout the week she'd told herself—about a hundred times and very firmly—that she would *not* let Michael's physical attributes get her distracted again. She would show him what a serious student she was. Not like some of the others, who seemed more enthusiastic about their teacher's good looks than about their art. And what's more, this week she would show him she could produce excellent work.

And so, after Michael had demonstrated how to use dry brushing to paint rough surfaces, she eagerly attacked her painting. Quickly she sketched a grouping of milkweed pods on an autumn field with the ease born of intimate familiarity with nature and life on the farm. Remembering how milkweed silk burst out of the pod and floated over the meadow, she began to paint the scene with loving care.

Michael wandered from table to table, giving individual assistance, but Shaylee found him standing behind her chair far more often than necessary. The milkweeds were coming to life quite nicely without him—thank you very much—and didn't need his constant scrutiny.

Suddenly she felt his hand on the back of her chair.

"Nice," he commented and followed this with a soft pat on the shoulder.

Shaylee squirmed and her back stiffened. *Nice?* How dare he use that word about her painting? She exhaled an exasperated sigh and slowly laid her brush on the table. With a scowl she turned to look up at him.

Michael's hand flew off the chair and he took a step back. "Nice," he repeated. "It's so—"

"Yes. Thank you," she snapped, and the scowl remained as she turned back to her work.

"I beg your pardon? Did I say something wrong?" Michael's voice was hard and cool.

Well, too bad if he was offended. He'd started it. *Nice!*

"No, of course not." Shaylee spoke to her paper but made sure he could hear the sarcasm lacing her words. "If you feel my work is *nice*, then," she shrugged, "what can I say but thank you?"

Before he could respond, Helena's whine interrupted their exchange.

"Michael, could you please come here," the redhead called from her corner. "See if anything can be done about this mess I've created."

Michael sauntered over to solve the problem, leaving Shaylee fuming. Nice. Ye gads, didn't that bring back memories of her brothers. *Nice work, Squirt.* And that condescending pat on her shoulder. He might as well have given her a dismissive smack on her bum. *Off you go, Munchkin.*

What was the matter with the man anyway, hovering near her continuously tonight? And when his hand had rested on the back of her chair, his fingers had brushed casually against her shoulder. Was that done on purpose? It bothered her the way the touch had spiraled down her spine, emerging as visible goose bumps on her skin. Stimulation of that kind she definitely did *not* need, not while she was trying her very best to show him what a capable artist she was.

"Why do you think he's over at our table so much?" Shaylee finally asked Marita, who toiled with heavy sighs of despair on her egg-shaped milkweed pods.

"Hah! Obviously you haven't figured out that he keeps coming here to subtly admire *my* work," Marita said with a straight face, swirling her brush in dark green wash. She dabbed at the forest in the background with an exaggerated flourish. "Why else do you think he'd be hovering behind *you* all evening? He's obviously trying to give the appearance he's actually not at all impressed with my painting. Clever man. He doesn't want my head to swell too much."

Shaylee's burst of laughter rang out over the room, causing all eyes to turn her way.

"Oops! Sorry." She lowered her head, shoulders still shaking. But the laughter lifted her spirits and she continued to work on her painting with a more cheerful attitude.

"You should have a stronger shade under that milkweed stem to anchor it. Right now it's too delicate. Looks like it's floating there."

Her body hadn't signaled his presence, perhaps because she'd been so totally absorbed in her work. But now his arm came to rest only inches away from hers, and some strange electricity seemed to draw her downy hairs toward his coarse ones. Perturbed, she moved her arm away.

"Use some Ultramarine Blue with a touch of Burnt Sienna," he said. "That will be better than . . . what is it you're using?"

"Ultramarine Blue and Burnt Sienna."

"Use more blue. It needs to be darker." To her ears the words were like a sharp command.

"Yes, sir." Shaylee held back a salute.

Michael turned and left without a word.

Darn. Did he have to be so terse? Shades of Mr. Crawley.

"Miss Palmer," the old teacher had said, his words accompanied by a very audible sigh. "The assignment distinctly specified you were to use three colours for this exercise. And I see you used only two."

"But, sir," Shaylee had protested, "I thought—"

"Miss Palmer, I would appreciate it if you would stop thinking for a change and follow the directives as given."

"Yes, *sir.*"

But the old teacher had already turned to go, missing her smart salute.

An hour later Shaylee emptied her water container and slipped her paints into a plastic bag. She gave one last, critical look at her painting. The work pleased *her* very much, and Marita was totally impressed with it. Michael, however, hadn't come near their table for the rest of the evening. Obviously he was annoyed with her. But it was his fault for being so dictatorial. Okay, so maybe she shouldn't have been so tetchy. She wished she could take back her quick-tempered reaction because now she had no idea what he thought of her work tonight.

But everyone else came to admire her milkweed

pods, and even Britney said the silk looked "ever so light and airy". But they were only students. None of them, except perhaps Britney, had produced anything worth writing home about. Now, if only Michael had commented favourably on her painting, she would have felt better.

But he didn't.

She knew he was ignoring her because of her sarcasm, and she probably deserved it, but still his bossy behavior had got to her. Chewing on her bottom lip, she picked up her materials, pulled on her coat, and then ran down the stairwell. She was anxious to get out into the fresh air and away from the source of her agitation.

In her high-heeled red boots Marita tiptoed precariously behind. "What's with you, anyway, rushing out like that?" she demanded when she caught up.

"I needed some fresh air."

They walked slowly toward the bus stop.

"You were so quiet and serious I didn't dare to say boo to you all evening," Marita said. "It was almost scary."

Shaylee shrugged. "Oh, I just wanted to concentrate on my work, that's all. I'm always like that when I'm painting."

But that didn't seem to convince Marita. "It looked to me like something was bugging you."

"Like what?" The words snapped out and immediately Shaylee was sorry. "I mean, what on earth could have been bugging me?"

Marita cast a sidelong glance at her. "The teacher, perhaps?"

Shaylee stopped in her tracks. Had it all been so obvious? Had everyone seen her irritation over Michael's comment? She tossed her head, defensively. "Well, you heard him. He criticized my shading. Too *delicate* for him. And he said my painting was nice. And he patted my back. I mean, if that's not a condescending put-down, I don't know what is." As she spoke, her voice rose in pitch, until the last word came out in an angry little squeak.

Marita came up beside Shaylee, a perplexed squint on her face. "What are you talking about? I didn't hear any put-downs from him."

"He said my painting was *nice*. You heard him." Shaylee scowled. She knew she sounded like a sullen kid. "And that pat he gave me. The only thing missing was, 'Atta girl Shaylee. Good job!'" She walked on in a defiant funk.

"Whoa! Hold on there." Marita started after Shaylee, waving her kid-gloved hand. "Michael's nice was a totally different sort of nice. Definitely not a condescending nice. I distinctly heard the Wow-factor in his voice."

Shaylee stopped and looked at Marita. "The Wow-factor?" Despite herself, a chuckle was building up inside her.

"Yes. Like, 'Wow! That's really *nice*.' There's a world of difference between that and your, 'Um . . . that's nice.' Pat, pat."

Shaylee burst out laughing as Marita clowned the actions. "You're sure you heard a Wow-factor?"

"Sure I'm sure."

"Okay, I guess I can see the difference," Shaylee admitted reluctantly. "And that ought to make me feel better. I think."

"If he said anything like that about *my* feeble efforts, I wouldn't feel just better. I would feel *terrific*," Marita stated emphatically.

Shaylee threw back her shoulders, her mood turning brighter. "You're right. In fact, I feel so much better I want to walk home and breathe in this fresh evening air. Coming?"

In her high heels Marita had trouble keeping up with Shaylee's brisk strides. "Slow down, already!" she called. "I didn't mean to make you feel *that* good."

Chapter Four

Holy Moley!" Marita hollered. She squinted at the name on the painting that hung in Shaylee's living room. "This is really *yours*?"

Shaylee nodded. "How many Shaylees do you know?" She deposited a plate of egg salad sandwiches on the table. They had decided to have lunch together and practise what they'd learned at the first two classes.

"So why are you taking art classes?" Marita came to the table, picked up a quarter sandwich and waved it toward the painting. "That is an absolute *masterpiece.*"

"That's very kind of you," Shaylee said. "But I'm not sure what your art critic credentials are, my otherwise learnèd friend." She took out some serviettes from a drawer. "Can you bring the plate of cut-up veggies to the table, please?"

"My credentials are that I know what I like when I see it," Marita retorted as she set the veggies on the table. "And I like that painting."

"Some people like pictures of Mickey Mouse, but that's not usually considered great art," Shaylee commented, pouring out two mugs of steaming coffee. She watched Marita scoop up three heaping spoonfuls of sugar and stir them into her coffee.

"Well, *I* happen to like pictures of Mickey Mouse," Marita said. "*And* sugar," she added with a grin.

Shaylee sighed. "I rest my case."

"But won't our teacher's eyes pop when he sees that masterpiece." Marita waved a celery stalk toward the living room.

"No!" Shaylee yelped, making Marita almost choke on her celery. "I'm not taking it to class."

Marita took a gulp of coffee after her coughing fit was over. "And why not, pray tell? You didn't really paint it? You copied someone's work? What?"

"No, it's nothing like that." Could she confide in her new friend and tell her about her deepest fears? Marita might think she was fishing for compliments. "I don't want to. The others might think I'm trying to show off or something."

"So you *do* think it's good, then? And you're protesting because you want to hear me sing its praises even more?"

Shaylee flushed at the look Marita sent her way. Just as she'd feared, Marita thought she was trying to snag her into flattery. "No, I do *not* want to hear praises," she countered. Well, naturally she wanted to hear praises, but she wished they'd come from an expert like Michael. And only if they were deserved. "Yes, *I* think it's good. But no one else has seen it. Except my family. My grandpa said it was great." But, then, what did he know? He never took an art lesson in his life. She swallowed. Dear Grandpa had meant well.

Would Marita make fun of her or would she understand? Shaylee decided to take the risk. "I'm scared to show it to Michael because . . . what if he thinks it's only a nice painting?"

Marita had put down her sandwich, signaling her readiness to listen. "Well, it is a nice painting."

"But I want him to think it's more than a nice painting. I want him to say it's *great*."

"And I'm sure he'll say it's great."

"I wish I knew." Scowling, Shaylee crunched on a carrot. "I know I can paint, but am I good enough to make a profession out of it? I paint all the time, and I'm totally passionate about it, but that doesn't mean what I'm producing is great art, does it?"

"Okay. So I can see this isn't simply a bashful act. But why? Anyone who can paint a masterpiece like that should know she's gifted."

"But I've never got a real expert's opinion," Shaylee insisted, now chewing on her thumbnail instead of the carrot. "I've been sort of a closet painter, if you know what I mean."

"Michael's an expert. He'll validate your work."

"But what if he only says it's *nice*?" Shaylee persisted. "I couldn't bear that."

Marita wagged a finger at Shaylee. "So what you're saying is, you'd rather hold onto your hope, rather than find out the truth. Like someone who's afraid he's got a serious disease and doesn't want to go to a doctor in case he gets bad news. Sooner or later, you're gonna have to face the music, my dear."

Marita's sympathetic voice reminded Shaylee her friend knew exactly how it felt to be rejected. After all, she'd been married to a man who left her for a younger, more svelte woman. If that didn't make a person fear rejection, nothing would.

"I know I'm being a coward, but I'm not ready to hear the bad news yet. I hope Michael didn't mean it when he said my work was nice—I mean, just nice. If he did, I think I'd stop painting forever." Shaylee lowered her head into her arms. "And I don't want to stop," she whispered miserably.

"And you're taking these classes because . . .?" Marita tapped Shaylee's arm to make her look up.

"Because . . ." Shaylee swallowed, and then, to cover up her discomfort, she turned to clowning. "Because I was hoping when Michael noticed how great I am he would fall down and genuflect before me, the great, newly discovered genius."

Marita laughed. "That's what you told me at the first class. I thought you were kidding, but you really meant it, didn't you?"

Shaylee felt her cheeks heat up. Her secret was out.

"I guess he wasn't impressed enough to bow down before you," Marita said. "So I can see why you're disappointed."

"You see? I *do* have a good reason for carrying this angst inside me." The words were said lightly but the angst inside her was very real.

Marita resumed her meal. "Didn't you take art in high school? Surely your teacher would have said something laudatory about your art."

"I only took it for one semester. And Old Mr. Crawley almost failed me." Shaylee grimaced. "The low marks he gave for my assignments made me totally rebellious, because I *knew* I was better than the others. But with his teaching method we had to paint endless colour wheels and stare at a white wall to see what colours we could see in it. And we had to do exactly what he said, no trying anything on our own." Her voice dropped an octave. "The great masters started out by copying the work of other masters. That was his favourite mantra. And he always pointed out things I should do differently. I started to hate art classes and dropped the subject at the end of the semester."

She'd often treated the simple art assignments as a joke. "I knew I could paint everyone else under the table even with my left hand. In fact, that's what I did when I fractured my right wrist in a fluky fall. I was racing with a couple of my brothers."

"Did you at least win?" Marita put in.

"No, I didn't. And until the cast came off, I behaved like the class clown. I drew and painted with my left hand and still produced work I knew was better than anyone else's in the class. But Mr. Crawley never said anything complimentary about my work. Maybe because he knew I was just goofing around. And even after the wrist was healed, I continued to use my left hand in class, simply to aggravate him." She sighed and took a sip of coffee. "I guess you could say I wasn't a very compliant student."

Marita nodded. "Sounds like you were a little brat. But I can also imagine how your behavior would have frustrated this Mr. Crawley. You know, maybe he was on your back all the time because he saw your potential and he was pushing you to try harder. Maybe he didn't want to give you good marks until you put forth an honest effort."

Shaylee bit into her sandwich. Could that be possible? Yes, she had certainly been a rebellious teenager, prone to silly behavior. She sighed and leaned her chin on her hand, which made chewing very awkward. "You may be right, Marita," she said ruefully. "And I'm sorry, Mr. Crawley, wherever you are, in heaven or still on this earth."

"Well, let sleeping Mr. Crawleys lie," Marita quipped. "No art classes in your community?"

"No. We lived in a pretty small farming community. There was nowhere for me to go and learn to paint." That still hurt.

Marita patted her shoulder. "Hey, at least now you can take lessons from a very handsome teacher. Makes Monday nights kind of interesting." She signaled the end of lunch by rising and picking up her plate.

Shaylee eyed her painting with a critical frown. "I wonder what Max Storm would say about that," she mused.

Marita put her plate into the sink. "Who's Max Storm?"

"He's the proprietor of the art gallery where I first saw Michael's paintings and fell in love with him."

Marita's eyes flew open.

Shaylee waved her hands in a panic. "Not *him. Them,*" she cried. "I meant the paintings." A fiery flush heated up her face. "I fell in love with them *paintings,*" she finished lamely.

Marita smiled smugly. "A Freudian slip, I believe that's called."

"Freudian nonsense, that's called," Shaylee retorted. "Will you stop insinuating there's something between Michael and me?"

Marita's face was a picture of innocence. "You said it, I didn't." She stepped into the hall to collect her paint bag. "But shouldn't we start our session, or are you going to gab all afternoon about Michael?"

"I wasn't gabbing about Michael." Shaylee collected the rest of the dishes and cutlery and took them to the sink.

Marita dumped her art materials on the table and picked up her latest work. She held it at arm's length.

"Hmmm. Could be improved a tad." She turned to Shaylee. "But to clarify my view on this situation, I think your art is good enough to hang in any gallery. And I think pretty soon Michael will figure out you can paint. I trust he has a brain, even if he is drop-dead gorgeous." She rolled her eyes. "And I tell you, I've been drooling over him for two whole weeks now."

Shaylee snorted. "Now who's gabbing about Michael?" But as she went to fill their water containers she had to admit—though not aloud—that their drop-dead gorgeous teacher hadn't been far from her thoughts, either. That smile had dimpled its way into her mind more times than she cared to admit. And the golden lights in his brown eyes had danced before her every time she closed her eyes at night.

"He's handsome, and there's no denying it," Shaylee said. "But he's definitely not my type." She didn't quite feel the disdain she tried to put into her words. "He's way too much aware of his good looks and seems to enjoy the attention of the ladies. Lothario. Isn't that what you called him? I agree, he's a real skirt-chaser."

Marita gave a loud guffaw. "Yeah, isn't he? And he can chase my skirts anytime."

Shaylee sprayed Marita with water droplets from her brush. "You're hopeless. But seriously, tomorrow night I'm going to produce something really good. Something that'll make him go, 'Wow!'."

And maybe then she would get up the nerve to show him that painting on the living room wall.

After work on Monday, Marita phoned and complained of feeling tired and listless. And at six-thirty, when Shaylee had just gathered up her art materials in readiness, Marita called again to say she had a full-blown head cold and would have to skip the class that evening.

She snuffled loudly into the receiver. "Or I bight drop something other than a blob of paint on by paper."

"That's too bad," Shaylee sympathized. "You get some rest now and drink plenty of fluids and stuff like that."

"Dank you."

Shaylee held the phone away from her ear as Marita sneezed.

"'Scuze be."

"I should feel sorry for you, but I can't help being happy because tonight there'll be one less woman to compete for the attentions of our handsome teacher." Shaylee hoped this joking would help her to remain laid-back and cool when he came around to see her work, and eradicate the excitement that had been building inside her all day. Of course it had nothing to do with her obsession with dimples, and everything to do with the simple joy of taking art lessons.

"Yes, well, enjoy it while you gan," Marita snuffled. "Next weeg you'll have to dake a back seat to be again."

Shaylee had to laugh. "I'll meet you with pistols at dawn before that."

Carrying her bag, she almost skipped all the way to the fruit market, so excited was she about her third art class. But as she climbed up the steep staircase, her steps slowed, and by the time she reached for the brass knob on the ugly green door, a feeling of vulnerability almost swept away her excitement. She would be in class without Marita to ease the annoying tension she seemed to feel in Michael's presence.

Britney glanced up somewhat ungraciously when

Shaylee entered, but managed to grimace with pity when Shaylee told everyone about Marita's condition.

"Glad *you* didn't catch it," Sue commented airily, while Helena tsk-tsked her concern.

The two men nodded from their corner; Bruce and Burt, or was it Burt and Bruce? And for once, instead of giggling, Tracy and Pauline clucked sympathetically about late winter colds. Only Peggy in her corner remained noncommittal.

As she took out her brushes and paints and prepared to follow Michael's lesson on weathered barn boards, Shaylee told herself tonight she would listen for the Wow-factor as Marita had advised. She would *not* get uptight if Michael used the dreaded n-word again, but she hoped Marita hadn't simply imagined the Wow-factor and it had really been there last week.

Tonight Michael seemed to be letting her paint in peace, to the point where Shaylee felt almost neglected. Was he still angry about last week, when she snapped at him? He'd greeted her cordially enough with a smile when she came in, but after that he hadn't come around even once to ensure she was getting started okay.

But despite—or perhaps because of—no teacher intervention, her work progressed well. The country scene unfolded with ease on her paper. An abandoned, weathered barn, with a rusty wagon wheel leaning against it. The odd thawed-out patch of ground, exposing dead grass and leaves told of the approaching spring. Shaylee was quite pleased with herself.

Then the hairs at the nape of her neck signaled Michael's presence even before she was aware that he had come over. His hand came to rest on the back of her chair and the knuckles lightly brushed her spine.

The effect of this almost nonexistent touch rippled through Shaylee with disconcerting intensity.

Michael leaned over her shoulder. "Some Sepia right there," he pointed with a long, slim finger, "will help define this tuft of grasses."

Ouch! Again he wasn't the least bit impressed with her painting. Never mind thinking it was brilliant. And here she'd been hoping so much to get a positive comment. But his next words dealt an even more crushing blow to her ego.

"Remember last time I talked to you about shading? These lines are too delicate and you need some defining. This over-delicacy seems to be something you perhaps need to pay attention to."

Her body reacted to him with disappointment mixed with anger but she bit back a retort. She'd come to these classes because he was a fabulous artist, and could one day decide her fate. Who was she to snap at him?

"Yes. Thank you for pointing that out." She tried her best to sound casual. "How about if I shade it with this mixture on my tray? I kind of like that colour, whatever it is."

"No. You should apply a touch of Sepia, as I said."

That sounded like a command and caused her hackles to bristle even more. He was totally unable to even consider a suggestion from a mere student. She looked up at him and gave him an insincere smile. Then, with exaggerated sweetness, she asked, "But surely there's more than one way to create that effect?"

Michael's jaw clenched, but she continued to smile. She wasn't going to be the one to snap.

"Yes, of course there is," he said evenly. "But I'm giving you the benefit of my years of experience and suggesting what I think will work best."

She heard the suppressed irritation in his voice but kept the smile pasted to her face. "You are right, Mr. Merrick." She made a point of sounding compliant. "Of course Sepia would work."

He relaxed and smiled back at her.

"But I'm sure I can get a similar effect touching up the grasses with this colour on my tray."

Michael's mouth drew into a hard line. "Probably," he said stiffly. "But as the teacher, I still stand by my opinion. Use Sepia."

Shaylee could almost hear the rest of the class holding its collective breath. She couldn't give in now.

"But would it be all right with you if I tried this, though? Since this is only a practice piece?"

"If you're such an expert, Miss Palmer, I wonder why you even bother coming to this class," Michael snapped and straightened up. His face was expressionless as he turned and continued his rounds.

Shaylee swirled her brush in the forbidden mixture on her paint tray, her shoulders hunched defiantly. So he didn't like her 'over-delicacy' as he called it? Well, too bad. It was her style. She liked to paint like that.

But would it hurt to touch up the scene as he'd suggested? Why not? She applied the colour neatly, and was even more pleased with her painting. So, Michael had been right, after all. The shading worked. But *not* necessarily Sepia.

As the evening drew to a close, it became very obvious Michael was deliberately keeping away from her. He hadn't come anywhere near her table since their rather bristly exchange. Shaylee lowered her brush and picked up her painting, holding it at arm's length. With her head cocked to one side she inspected it carefully. Well, *she* thought it had turned out well, no matter what he said, or didn't say.

"Looks fine." Again Michael had come up behind her so quietly, he caught her off guard.

"I thought you didn't like it without the Sepia." The words burst out of her before she could hold them back.

"I didn't say that. I only gave a suggestion to improve one tiny aspect of it. It's a nice painting for someone who's only been dabbling on her own."

Nice painting? No matter how she tried to imagine it, she couldn't hear a Wow-factor. Dabbling, was she? Frowning, she looked up, ready to respond, but found his head bent alarmingly close. His lips were there, only an inch from her mouth. And then, just for a second they brushed against hers.

Of all the nerve! Shaylee quickly ducked her head, but not before she'd seen his eyes light up. That helped her regain her composure and reinforced her resolution to curb her temper. She would not explode. But she would also let him know she wasn't going along with his flirtatious games.

"Well, that *also* was nice," he murmured close to her ear.

As Shaylee turned to glare at him, infuriating dimples appeared on his cheeks. "If that's another *nice* comment on my work, then I thank you," she muttered through clenched teeth, relieved Marita wasn't here to witness this.

"Little Fairy Princess," he mockingly whispered. "I didn't realize you felt this way about me." His head bent so close she could feel his breath on her hair.

Shaylee sprang up and, with a loud scrape, pushed her chair back against his stomach. "Mr. Merrick, I think we have something to discuss after class," she hissed, picking up her water container. "Now, please excuse me." She brushed past him on her way to the sink. If only she were brave enough to fling the colourful contents of the dish at his grinning face.

By the time she returned to her seat, Michael was already at the other end of the room, whistling softly. Whistling! Of all the—! She took a few deep breaths, making a deliberate effort to calm down her pulse, which had shot way up.

How could he have the audacity to kiss her, right here in class? Did he already consider her one of his groupies? And then have the nerve to waltz off, whistling and pretending everything was simply tickety-boo. If she were to continue coming to class, this issue would have to be resolved immediately. She couldn't allow him to think for a moment that she appreciated his uninvited attentions. Maybe the other women were thrilled to play hanky-panky with him, but Shaylee Palmer was definitely *not*.

When the class was over, Shaylee took extra care packing up her painting and spent considerable time at the sink, rinsing her brushes and giving her water dishes a vigorous, unnecessary scrubbing. She couldn't help overhearing Michael making plans with Britney to go to her place for dinner again on the weekend. She made a face at the chrome faucet. Didn't the man ever eat at home?

Some of the women seemed to linger around forever and cast sidelong glances her way. Shaylee became increasingly embarrassed, thinking they might see through her deliberate stalling, but by hook or by crook, she was determined to be the last one to leave. Her concerns had to be addressed. Tonight. The man needed to be set straight on how she felt about his flirtatious behavior.

At last everyone was gone. Shaylee shrugged into her coat and pulled on her boots. Then, straightening, she beamed her eyes up—way up—directly at Michael. He was leaning against the doorframe waiting for her, arms folded casually across his broad chest.

His eyes twinkled roguishly, almost managing to fluster her, but she swallowed hard and began. "Mr. Merrick—"

"Michael." He cut her off nonchalantly. "My name is Michael."

"Mr. Merrick," she went on as though she hadn't heard him. "I want to—"

"Michael," he interrupted again.

Her stomach tightened, but she tried to ignore his deliberate attempt to rattle her. "I want to tell you I find your uninvited attentions very unpleasant. And what's more—"

One eyebrow raised quizzically. "Exactly what attentions might they be?" His seemingly innocent question infuriated her. "You realize, as the teacher it's my duty to pay attention to each of my students."

With an iron hand on her temper, Shaylee kept her cool, although the blood boiled in her veins. "I thought your duty as a teacher was to help your students produce better paintings, not to . . ." She didn't want to put a name to the action.

"Yes?"

The darned man sounded amused. This was not the apologetic reaction she'd expected. The playful golden lights in his eyes were getting her all muddled up, and she regretted ever having started this.

"Not to k-kiss them in the middle of the class," She

finally blurted out, dismayed at the way her voice caught at the word "kiss". Feeling more flustered by the second, she decided it best to drop the whole thing and get out of Dodge before she made a bigger mess of things.

"Good night, Mr. Merrick," she snapped haughtily and with her chin up, she turned to go. At least her actions would show suitable indignation, where her words had failed miserably.

But suddenly she found her arm in an iron grip. "Now, wait a moment, Miss Palmer." Michael swung her around to face him. "I think we ought to clear up a little misunderstanding here. You know very well it was *you* who kissed *me* tonight in class."

Her eyes flew open, to match her mouth. "How *dare* you even suggest that," she cried, trying unsuccessfully to wrench her arm free. "I would *never* do such a thing."

"Well, I would." His voice was smooth as silk. "But this time I didn't. You raised your lips up to mine."

"I certainly did *not*!"

"Are you saying I kissed you?"

The naked ceiling light disappeared from view as he lowered his head. Shaylee caught the laughter in his eyes, before they closed.

"Like this?" he murmured, his lips hovering close, only a breath away from hers.

She could see a speck of Raw Sienna on his cheek before her eyes also closed. And then it happened again. For the second time that night his lips were on hers.

But this time they lingered. And in spite of herself, despite everything, she wanted them to stay. When he raised his head, the bare bulb danced dizzily in her eyes, as it had the first time they had met with that clash of heads.

"See? Again you raised your lips to mine," Michael said softly.

"No!" Her voice was a mere rasp, barely audible. "You're wrong." But her eyes had been closed, so how could she be sure?

"Let's try it again," he suggested. "And this time let's both be more vigilant about who approaches who first." He sounded earnest but it was obvious he was laughing inside. "We've got to settle this once and for all."

"You're crazy." Shaylee tore herself from his arms, which had somehow found their way inside her coat and around her waist. She swung around and took off, storming down the stairs with a clatter of boots.

"You can't go out like that, sweetheart." Michael's teasing voice echoed in the stairwell. "Button up your coat and put your scarf and hat on. It's cold out there."

Shaylee turned to glare up at him. "I'll go out as I please, Mr. Merrick," she called icily. "You may tell me how to paint, but *not* how to dress."

She slammed the door shut. This was the last time she would ever darken *that* doorway again.

Chapter Five

Slowly Michael took his jacket off the coat rack and slipped an arm into a sleeve. Shaylee didn't seem to give a damn about his advice. So much for any idea of mentoring.

But the little vixen *had* to know she was good. She had to. And she probably wanted to goad him into praising her work to the skies. Well, he wasn't about to fall all over himself flattering her. Although, dammit all, tonight's painting didn't look like a practice piece. It was good enough to frame right then and there.

And last week she'd used such a delicate touch to paint the strands of milkweed silk bursting out of the dry pods. She'd made them look so soft and airy he almost could have imagined them taking off and floating around the room.

Kind of like her soft hair. With her head bent earnestly over her work, he'd had the crazy urge to sink his fingers into the blond curls, to see if they were as silky as they looked.

But when he'd commented on her work she'd become snippy. What exactly had he said to her? *Nice*, if he recalled correctly. Was that it? She didn't like him call her work nice? Well, if she hadn't interrupted him

with her huffy thank you, she would have heard him
compliment her on the delicate softness of her brush-
work and the way she'd succeeded in creating the
rough texture of the pod.

But now she could damn well stew in her own
juices, the little sharp-clawed kitten.

But what about that kiss tonight? Of all the women
in the class, he never would have expected *her* to ini-
tiate it. Or could it have been him, after all? Damned
if he knew for sure. Maybe he *had* been the one who
spanned the last inch to her upturned face. Her mouth
was so irresistible, possibly his lips had gravitated
down to touch it out of pure need.

But he could have sworn it was *she* who'd raised
her lips to his.

Michael closed the studio door behind him and
started down the stairs. Whatever the mystery behind
the kiss, there was no mystery in the chill in her voice,
nor in the ominous sound of finality in the explosive
slam of the door when she left.

"I told you I'm *not* going to that class ever again,"
Shaylee said firmly. "I said so a week ago and I meant
it." Ensconced in the armchair in her blue bathrobe,
she sat, arms folded defiantly on her chest. Her feet,
deep in fuzzy pink slippers, were planted on the coffee
table, to make it absolutely clear she wasn't about to
go anywhere tonight.

Marita continued to argue. "But you've already paid
for the lessons." She waited, leaning against the doorframe, her art bag slung over one shoulder.

"I don't care."

"But I got all dressed up to walk. You heard me,
w-a-l-k to class tonight. And I don't want to walk by

myself."

"So take the bus," Shaylee retorted heartlessly. "I think I have made it quite clear that I am not going."

"Well, I thought you'd change your mind when you saw me all set to brave the wintry blizzards," Marita grumbled. "Besides, I can't imagine what could have happened last week that was so terrible you'd want to quit."

"No, you can't imagine." Shaylee could feel her cheeks heat up at the memory of the kisses.

"What is it?" Marita asked. "Are you blushing or do you have a fever?"

To hide her flushed face, Shaylee reached for the TV remote on the coffee table. "Perhaps I *do* have a touch of something or other. Please tell Mr. Merrick I have a sore throat. That's not exactly a lie, either, because I'm quite prone to sore throats."

"Prone to?"

"Not that I have one right now," she hastily explained. "But I often get them in October or November, so technically I *could* have one. It's still winter after all, and . . ." Yes, absolutely she *did* sound ridiculous. No question about that.

Marita showed no sympathy. "I think I understand. You get sore throats in October, but you don't have one now, because it's March, but you *could* have one. Okay, I'll lie for you, but I won't announce your resignation till you've had time to reconsider. Though personally I don't see why you're letting our charming teacher get to you."

Shaylee almost exploded out of the chair. "Our charming teacher has nothing whatsoever to do with it!" What a bald-faced lie. Of course he did. Everything. But she wasn't about to let her friend wrangle the truth out of her. She never wanted to see this man again. Not in this life. Or even in the next.

"I thought you were leaving," she muttered, settling back in a sullen funk.

At that Marita withdrew. "Good night, little ray of sunshine. Have a lovely sore throat," she said closing the door behind her.

The evening dragged on endlessly. The TV had nothing to offer that appealed to her and the book she'd been reading with such great interest the night before, now turned into a bore. She wandered around the apartment, giving a passing thought to answering her e-mail, sewing on a missing button, and dusting. It took no time at all to dismiss them as dull, duller, and no way!

This was crazy. Although Marita was telling everyone in class she was sick, it didn't mean she actually had to act the part inside her own apartment. Why shouldn't she go out for a breath of fresh air, for goodness' sake? A brisk walk would help her sleep more peacefully, without thinking constantly about what happened last Monday. Having her mind wrapped around Michael's kisses was totally ludicrous. Enough of that, already.

She kicked off the slippers and took out her boots. Dressed warmly for an unseasonably cold evening, she emerged a few minutes later on the sidewalk and drew in deep breaths of the invigorating night air.

The calendar had already pronounced it as dead, but winter was still trying desperately to fight against its final demise. After a week of milder weather, it had turned chilly again and light snow was falling. With sparkling whiteness, it lay on the mounds of frozen, dirty slush along the curbs. The salt trucks had been out earlier and the roads were now wet with melting snow. At almost nine o'clock, the streets appeared deserted. On a night like this everyone was probably snuggled in front of a TV, or absorbed in some computer game.

Exulting in the joy of moving her limbs, Shaylee set off at a brisk pace. Then, in a burst of energy she broke into a run, but soon the heavy boots slowed her down to a jog. A block or two later, even that became laborious and once more she settled into a comfortable walk. By now her cheeks and nose were red, but warm, her fingers and toes toasty. The vigorous walk was already having the desired effect and she hadn't thought of that annoying man for almost two blocks.

Michael closed the door of the studio, took the stairs down two at a time, and stepped out onto the sidewalk. He pulled up the collar of his black bomber jacket and headed for his car, parked half a block away. The evening had been a disaster. Shaylee hadn't come. Naturally he didn't believe a word of the story Marita had spun about Shaylee's sore throat. Of course her absence had everything to do with what happened between them last week.

He only hoped she hadn't been put off for good and quit the class because, honestly, he hadn't meant for the kisses to happen. In fact, he still wasn't clear exactly how it all had come about.

The kiss had been so brief, but so sensual, that even now all hell broke loose inside him at the thought. In intensity it didn't compare with the hundreds he'd experienced with any number of women, but its fleeting sweetness had replayed over and over in his mind during the past week, catching him unguarded.

Michael reached his car and touched the handle to unlock the door. She was something special, all right. He'd seen it the moment she walked into the studio. And she was a damned stubborn little pixie, too. He chuckled, remembering how she'd used the mix of colour off her tray, instead of following his advice to use Sepia. And the shading had turned out fine. Not that he'd given her the satisfaction of telling her so, because the defiant minx didn't need his praises. She was cocky and confident enough about her art to question and contradict his instruction, so why should he feed her vanity?

He got into his car and was about to push the start button, when a small figure in a dark overcoat sped by on the sidewalk.

Shaylee. He got out and slammed the door shut after him. Pressing the remote, he took off after her.

When he got close, he reached out to touch her shoulder, and heard her gasp in alarm. She whirled around to face him and looked relieved when she recognized him.

"Michael! You scared me half to death."

"I'm sorry. I didn't mean to frighten you. I should have called out to warn you."

She frowned, now looking more confused than frightened. "Wh-what are you doing here?"

In the glow of the streetlamps she looked like a little troll, all trussed up in heavy winter gear. Michael smiled. "That's what I was going to ask you. I was just about to drive off when you raced by. I thought maybe you were coming to class a couple of hours late."

Under the streetlight's glow, Shaylee's eyes flashed with embarrassment before she dropped her gaze, staring awkwardly at her boots. "I didn't notice I'd walked this far," she muttered.

Michael felt sorry for her and to ease the situation he asked, "So how are you? Marita said you weren't feeling well."

"Oh, I thought a walk might do me good," Shaylee threw out casually, not answering his question.

At least she wasn't trying to get out of the embarrassing situation by lying. "Looks like it did. You were steaming by at such a clip I had a hard time catching up with you."

"Yes, I feel great now." She clapped her mittened hands briskly.

"I'm glad. But could I still offer you a ride home? It might not be wise to exert yourself *too* much." He couldn't help teasing her.

She grimaced. Obviously she'd heard the laughter in his voice and knew her story about her sore throat was shot full of holes. "Thanks, but I was actually planning to take a nice long walk. Makes me feel so much better, you know."

"Could I walk you home, then?" Michael held his breath, hoping she was willing to forget what had happened at the last class. For a few seconds Shaylee seemed to hesitate, but when she grinned shyly up at him he exhaled with relief.

"Yes, I'd like that," she replied. "But then you'd have to walk back to your car and that's probably more walking than you were planning to do tonight."

"To tell you the truth, I wasn't planning on doing *any* walking tonight." He reached into his pockets and pulled out a toque and a pair of gloves. "But luckily I always come prepared. Never know when I might meet a lady in distress who needs to be walked home." He raked the long hair off his forehead and pulled on the toque.

"I accept, as long as you can keep up with me."

Shaylee turned to walk back toward her apartment building and Michael fell in step beside her.

"I think a brisk walk will do me a world of good after being cooped up inside all day," he said. All evening he'd been kicking himself, afraid he would never see Shaylee again and here he was, having a friendly conversation with her.

"This will give me a chance to pick your brains and get a make-up lesson for the one I missed tonight," she said.

That sounded very positive! "Well, you didn't miss too much," he told her. "We were still working on rough textures." Picking up a batch of freshly fallen snow he formed it into a snowball and tossed it at a telephone pole. He missed. "Don't you dare laugh."

He scooped up some more snow, packed it into a ball and handed it to her. "I bet you can't do any better."

"Don't get me started on throwing snowballs at poles," Shaylee warned. "Because then I'm compelled to stay until I make a strike. That could take a few hours."

"Well, I'm in no hurry. Are you?"

"No, but don't say I didn't warn you." Shaylee took the snowball and turned it around in her mittens. "We may still be here when the stores open up in the morning." She took careful aim and threw. The ball hit the pole with a splat. She clapped her mittens together to shake off the snow.

"I'll never believe you again," Michael exclaimed. "You pretend to be a total neophyte and instead you're an expert marksman."

Shaylee laughed. "Believe me, that was a complete fluke."

"Yeah, sure it was." Michael picked up more snow and threw another ball at the pole. He missed. He made another snowball. Missed again. And another. Missed once more.

"We're running out of fresh snow," Shaylee observed.

He could tell she was trying not to laugh. The wet snow was seeping through his leather gloves, soaking them thoroughly.

"We're not leaving, even if it takes till morning," Michael huffed and formed another snowball. This time he made a hit. "Do *not* clap," he warned. "Do *not* say good. That would be way too condescending."

"How about if I pat you on the shoulder and say nice?"

"Touché." He could hear the teasing in her voice. Of course he remembered. "Let's say we're even now." With difficulty he tugged off his wet glove and extended his hand. "Shake?"

Shaylee pulled off her snowy mitten and took his hand. Even though her hand was cool, her touch produced a warmth that streamed right through him. Like that kiss had done. Did she feel anything? She quickly pulled her hand away and slipped on her mitten, while looking at her boots almost shyly. Perhaps the touch had had a similar effect on her.

They continued to walk at a leisurely pace, chatting about the missed lesson. From time to time Michael stopped to illustrate his words by sketching with a stick on a patch of fresh snow.

"You did a nice job with those milkweed pods," he

told her.

She looked up, and the pleasure shining in her eyes made him smile. Luckily she didn't seem to have noticed he'd inadvertently used the forbidden n-word.

"You think so?" She sounded surprised.

"Yes, I thought the silk was almost ready to fly around the room." He regretted not having said anything about it to her in class. She certainly deserved to hear it.

"Oh," was all she said, but he could detect her happiness from the way her step became more bouncy and light. "Maybe it's because I'm on such intimate terms with milkweed pods," she then added.

"How's that?"

"I come from a farm near Kitchener and grew up with barn boards and milkweed pods and other rough surfaces."

"Kitchener? I sometimes go there in the summer and take pictures of the Mennonite farmers driving their buggies. Very picturesque folk."

"Many of our neighbours are Mennonites." The way she said that sounded like she was defending them.

Michael stopped. "I'm sorry. I didn't mean to sound like some rubber-necking urbanite who comes to ogle at the locals and snap pictures."

"You didn't." She took the stick from his hand and quickly sketched a horse and buggy on a patch of fresh snow. "It's beautiful there, and I love to paint the countryside. I want to be able to do it justice."

Michael looked down at the face before him. Under the streetlight her face glowed with earnest enthusiasm. "Come to classes and develop your technique, and I'm sure in time you'll be able to do exactly that."

It seemed like their rather confrontational beginning

was having a fresh new start. Walking beside her, Michael was very conscious of the way her arm brushed against his from time to time. But it wasn't only being with her and talking with her about art that made him happy. It was the realization that he was walking with a beautiful woman and yet it all felt so friendly and companionable. He wouldn't have minded if their friendship could develop into something a bit more romantic, but he knew this farm girl wouldn't be interested in a passing fling. And anything more permanent didn't even register as a faint blip on his radar. Reluctantly he pushed the thought of last Monday's sweet kisses out of his mind.

Shaylee pointed at the display window of a ladies' clothing store. "If those fashions are to be believed, spring has already arrived, but this weather's telling me they're lying."

"Which reminds me," Michael put in. "I asked the class tonight if anyone would be interested in coming to take pictures of trees in Wilket Creek Park on Saturday. It's a chance to see the basic shapes of the various trees while the branches are all bare. We'll be meeting at the north end of the parking lot at ten."

"I think that sounds great," she said. "Yes, I'd like to come." She grinned up at him. "I've often painted and sketched by myself around my home, but having an expert along to explain things will be a real bonus."

"I'm glad. I was afraid that after last Monday you might never want to come to class again."

Shaylee grimaced. "Let's not mention last Monday again. Okay? Let's not even think about it."

But Michael knew that would be impossible. Maybe she would never think of it again, but as for him—

"Hey, speaking of paints," she burst out, as if trying

to make sure the previous topic was finished and done for. "Who thought up all those weird names for paints?"

She began to tell him the funny ideas she and Marita had thought up.

Michael burst out laughing at the slop bucket full of Brown Madder.

"And I think the most passionate paint is R-r-raw Sienna," Shaylee concluded, strongly rolling the r-sound.

He chuckled. "I hate to disillusion your romantic soul, but the names have very prosaic roots. Umber, for example, comes from the earth and gets its colour from the manganese and iron oxides."

Shaylee snorted in dismay. "How dull. I prefer my own interpretations."

"So do I," he admitted. "And from now on I'll become hot with passion whenever I swirl my brush in R-r-raw Sienna."

"And become nauseated when using Brown Madder?"

"Definitely. Though I'll always feel bad the reputation of a perfectly good paint has been ruined."

They walked on, until suddenly Shaylee exclaimed, "Oh my goodness, here's my building."

Michael was disappointed. "Already? I thought you lived much farther than this."

Shaylee eyed the apartment building suspiciously. "I'm *sure* I live much farther than this. I think it must have sneaked up to meet us."

They stood at the front door, neither making a move to go anywhere. Michael knew he should simply say good night and be on his way, but he didn't want the evening to end. Not yet. It had been so wonderful to talk with her like friends.

Shaylee's hand groped for the door handle, never quite reaching it. He hoped it also indicated her unwillingness to call it a night.

He wanted very much to wrap her up in his arms, overcoat and all, and feel again the sweet tenderness of that kiss. He was afraid to close the gap between them but the need to touch her was intense. So instead he pulled off one glove and reached out to gently run his finger down her reddened cheek. It was warm and smooth. "I'm so glad I ran into you tonight. Or ran after you, to be more precise."

She laughed at his words. "Me too."

They couldn't just stand there in the cold night air forever, or she would really come down with a cold. He held out his hand. "I enjoyed our walk."

Hesitantly she took off her mitten and slipped her hand into his. "Yes, I did, too," she murmured.

For a while they stood, hand in hand, and he couldn't believe the sweet feeling this simple touch produced in him. He would have called it sensual, except it was just a handshake. An innocent handshake. But he felt it deep in his heart where he hadn't felt much for some time. This little Fairy of the Field had a way of affecting him in the most surprising ways. This could get dangerous.

"Good night, Shaylee." He gave her hand a squeeze and then reluctantly released it. "I'll see you Saturday."

After she went in, Michael stood there, gazing at the closed door. Why was he feeling like this? It had never been necessary to remind himself of the fact that art was, and always would be, his first commitment. He wanted no strings and no responsibilities.

So why did he now have to review the firm rules he'd

set for himself after the divorce? Only casual affairs allowed. And this little farm girl definitely didn't fall into the casual affair category. Not by a country mile.

He turned and began the return trip back to his car, but somehow the distance seemed twice as long without her.

Inside her apartment Shaylee removed her overcoat which, standing close to Michael a moment ago, had begun to feel almost superfluous. She glanced at herself in the hall mirror and touched her cheek where the touch of his hand had caused a pleasant warmth to course through her and had brought a glowing colour to her face. She smiled at her reflection. Michael had been so friendly tonight. So easy to talk to. Exactly the way she'd imagined the artist named Michael Merrick would be when she had first seen his work at The Four Winds Gallery. Except the real Michael was a lot handsomer than anything she had imagined.

It was a relief to discover tonight that his paintings hadn't lied, after all.

But it was the positive feedback he'd given her that made her heart beat with happiness. He had actually said she'd done a nice job with the milkweed pods. Even though he'd used the dreaded n-word she felt there had been some of the Wow-factor in his words, which Marita had told her to look out for. And although he hadn't said she had talent, coming from a professional artist like him, even those "nice" comments were welcome.

Shaylee thought of the gentleness in his voice. She'd never heard him speak in that tone before, and it made the colour rise onto her cheeks anew.

With a sigh, she flopped into the armchair and

switched on the TV. If only tonight's easy friendship would continue. She looked at the screen, but instead of the evening news she saw only the disarming dimples that had laughed with her tonight.

But what about all the *stuff* that went on in class? And obviously outside the class, too. That, she told herself, was not her business. It was totally beside the point and didn't mean he couldn't still be a wonderful person and a great artist. Some men were just natural charmers and juggled women like oranges.

But despite her effort to reason logically, that thought produced an unpleasant taste in her mouth.

Since she'd already prepaid the lessons, she might as well continue them. Maybe, just maybe, one of these days Michael would look at her work in class and say, "That's great, Shaylee! Girl, you've really got *talent*." Then she would bring that painting from off the wall for him to see.

And that was the *only* thing that was important.

Chapter Six

Shaylee stood on the assigned parking lot. Alone. Marita had adamantly refused to come along for the Saturday outing. Something about plowing ankle-deep in slush not being her thing.

Unfortunately, with fewer buses running on the weekend, Shaylee had waited over half an hour before one had come ambling along. So by the time she arrived at the park, almost forty-five minutes late, everyone had already disappeared into the valley. She couldn't blame them. They probably thought she'd changed her mind, or had slept in. She would have called Michael, but had forgotten her phone at home, as usual, so there was no way she could let him know she would be late.

The weather was quite mild for a change. The mercury had pushed its way nicely above the freezing mark and Shaylee wore jeans and only a light jacket. She'd also put on rubber boots, for she knew the snow would be getting wetter as the day warmed up. And of course the creek was there, with places that might be the right depth for wading. Impossible to resist.

At first she didn't worry about not being able to locate the group, because it had snowed lightly during the night and there were plenty of fresh tracks that were easy to follow. Unfortunately, as she began to inspect them more closely, she discovered they fanned out in every conceivable direction. So obviously not all the cars in the parking lot belonged to people from the art class.

Perplexed, she stood among the footprints and for a moment she considered returning home. But the park, sparkling in the sunshine, was irresistible. The evergreens were dusted lightly with snow and even the smallest twig glittered. Shaylee slipped on her sunglasses and decided to spend a few moments by herself taking pictures with her camera. If they turned out, maybe she could use some of them as inspiration for winter scenes.

She slung her backpack, containing a thermos and a sandwich, over one shoulder and wandered into the peaceful ravine, wanting to get as far as possible from the parking lot and any other signs of civilization. As she descended the embankment toward the river, she took care not to end up sliding down the slippery slope on her behind. She pushed through the bushes and reached the river that half-slumbered in its willow-fringed bed. The water level was down, leaving a narrow path along the edge for her to maneuver along with care.

She continued on, stumbling now and then on the slippery rocks and grabbed onto helpful branches for support. When she came to a clearing she stopped. The shore was level and wide at this point, and covered with icy pebbles. The embankment to her left was thick with young maples and poplars, with the fawn-coloured leaves of a beech adding a dash of contrast to the white and gray landscape.

Here and there the dark and sluggish water of the stream was veneered by transparent ice. The submerged rocks and bits of flotsam were capped by little mounds of icy snow that looked like giant marshmallows in the river. Shaylee kicked loose some small stones and began to throw them at the round snowcaps.

She was so absorbed in her target practice she didn't hear the group of people approach from behind, until a familiar, high-pitched laughter pierced the stillness around her.

"Well, if it isn't Shaylee, throwing stones into the water. How charming."

It sounded like Britney. Shaylee turned slowly to face the intruders. Michael, with an entourage of ladies, made his way down the treed embankment, slowly negotiating the slippery rocks and boulders, with Britney using his arm for support. At last they reached the spot where Shaylee stood, still clutching an icy stone in her mitten.

Michael grinned at her. He was wearing jeans, and his open bomber jacket revealed a cream cable-knit sweater. "I hope you aren't planning to throw that at me."

With a short, mirthless laugh, Shaylee tossed the stone into the river and dismissed her activity with a shrug. "I planned to take some pictures," she explained. "But I got carried away." She reached for her backpack that lay against a rock. "I got here late and couldn't find you."

"Then it's lucky we found *you*," Michael said. "We haven't taken any pictures either because we decided to walk first to see what the ravine had to offer today."

"It's been a great walk," Sue said, while Tracy and

Pauline nodded enthusiastically.

"Absolutely divine," Helena agreed. "We were going to stop for a snack as soon as we found a suitable spot. This looks fine, doesn't it, Michael?"

Michael raised a questioning eyebrow. "As long as Shaylee doesn't mind us intruding?"

"Not at all." Shaylee gave a broad sweep with her arm. "You're welcome to have a picnic on my estate. The facilities are a bit primitive, but maybe you could sit on some of my logs and rocks?"

"Thanks. You're a most congenial hostess." Michael took a thermos out of his backpack and removed his jacket. "We waited for you for about fifteen minutes until the ladies began to get impatient."

He spread his jacket onto a log and bowed gallantly to Britney. "Milady?"

Britney waltzed over and with a little wiggle, placed her slim bottom, covered in skin-tight jeans, on the coat. The others sat here and there on large rocks and stumps, using their backpacks for cushions against the dampness.

Shaylee took out her thermos and, sitting on her backpack, leaned back against a cold tree trunk. She poured black, steaming coffee into the thermos cap and took a sip. Her day had been much more enjoyable before this crew intruded. But, heck, surely the park was big enough for everyone. Even Britney.

"But where will *you* sit, Michael?" Britney asked, when Michael started to move toward Shaylee.

"If you don't mind, Shaylee, I'll share your tree." He stood, leaning back against it before she could answer.

Britney patted the space beside her on the log. "Oh, but you'd be much more comfortable sitting here!"

"I'm fine." Michael's reply was polite but firm, but

clearly Britney didn't want to relinquish him too easily.

"Michael has agreed to come for dinner tonight," she announced, laying claim to him with her words, if not with her hands. Her eyes narrowed into slits as she looked at Shaylee.

Michael unscrewed his thermos cap and filled it with hot coffee. "You're kind to invite a starving artist for a home-cooked meal," he said. "How could I refuse?"

Sitting at the foot of the tree, Shaylee could see only Michael's denim-clad legs and brown hiking boots as he stood beside her, but she felt the nearness of his entire, masculine body. Too strongly.

"You're very lucky to have a friend like Britney, who likes to cook." She tried her best to sound more sincere than she felt.

Michael disregarded her comment and aimed his words to her ears alone. "I was so disappointed I didn't see you when we got here. I wanted to wait longer, but . . ."

Shaylee thought back to the walk they'd shared on Monday night and longed to believe his words. But having observed the way he'd come strutting along like a handsome rooster with his retinue of clucking hens, it was easy to doubt his sincerity.

Shrugging, she tossed off the dregs of coffee from her cup and got up, stretching. "I'd like to take some photos before the morning is completely gone," she said. "I have some things to do this afternoon." Like what, for example?

"Let's get a move on, then," Michael called. "Ladies, time to take out the cameras."

Everyone scurried to pack up and find their cameras. Michael directed their attention to a maple tree, high on the opposite bank, its dark shape etched against the azure blue sky.

"You notice the limbs growing out from the trunk are heavy," Michael pointed out. "And each time they branch out, they become lighter and lighter. Kind of like your blood vessels."

"Ugh! Don't talk of blood, Michael, please," Britney cried with a shiver. "We're supposed to be taking pictures of trees, not having an anatomy lesson."

Michael shrugged. "I was only making a comparison to help you visualize."

"Well, you helped me feel nauseous."

Shaylee's upper lip curled in disdain. Ridiculous. She was glad Michael only turned and walked on.

They stopped here and there in the ravine to photograph other varieties of trees—oak, birch, poplar—while Michael drew their attention to the distinguishing characteristics of each one in turn.

A twisted, ice-coated branch in the middle of the stream caught Shaylee's eye. The sun's rays had transformed it into a glittering glass sculpture.

"Oh, look how beautiful!" she exclaimed. "I want to take a picture of it close up." Gingerly she stepped onto the frozen, snow-covered creek, and then advanced cautiously, testing the strength of the ice with each step.

"Listen, maybe you shouldn't—" Michael began, but just then the ice under Shaylee's feet cracked, and she froze on the spot.

"I think you're right," she said nervously. Slowly she began to turn around, but all at once the ice gave way. With a shrill scream she landed on her bottom in the river. The water barely came to her waist, but she could feel it penetrate her clothing, flow into her boots, pierce her body with deadly coldness. Madly she tried to scamper up, but couldn't find a foothold on the slippery rocks and she fell again, this time onto her side. Now only her head and one shoulder remained dry. The camera slipped from her grip and sank into the black water.

Oblivious to everything except the urgent need to escape from the freezing water, Shaylee scrambled onto her hands and knees while the icy cold pierced her body. But then she felt strong hands help her onto her feet, while Michael's voice, penetrating through her panic, quietly reassured her. She slipped and skidded, but with his steadying arm around her Shaylee remained upright and managed to reach the shore.

There she was immediately swept up into Michael's arms.

"Please call a cab for yourself," he said to Britney. "You've got a phone with you, haven't you? Or one of you others please give Britney a ride home. The dinner date's cancelled."

He started up the embankment with long strides, carrying Shaylee with ease, despite her heavy, saturated clothing.

"Don't worry about a thing, Michael," Shaylee heard Helena's concerned voice calling. "Just get her home quickly."

When they reached the open, unprotected parking lot, Shaylee began to shiver and her teeth chattered uncontrollably. The wind blew right through her soggy clothes and threatened to turn her into another ice sculpture.

Michael put her down. "You've got to get into my car right away. Come on, run," he urged her, forcing her heavy, sloshing feet to move.

"I have to g-get h-home," Shaylee stuttered through clenched teeth. But even as she stammered out the words, she knew it would be ridiculous to even think of taking a bus in her condition.

"I'm taking you to my place." Michael's tone brooked no discussion. "I live very close."

The icy wind killed any thoughts of resistance and Shaylee let herself be bundled into Michael's car and wrapped up in his jacket. He removed her sodden boots, drained the water out of them and tucked a car blanket around her feet.

"Your c-coat will g-get wet," Shaylee pointed out.

Michael jumped in and started the car. "It's all right. I've got a dryer."

Having stood for over two hours on the parking lot, the vehicle was cold, but at least now Shaylee was sheltered from the bitter wind. In the few minutes before the heater began to blow hot air, she sat stiffly, trying in vain to prevent the cold, clammy clothes from touching her skin.

They soon reached Michael's home, a turn-of-the-century, two-story redbrick semi. Once inside, he led her directly to his bedroom on the second floor and started a bath in the adjoining bathroom.

"Get into the tub as soon as possible and have a good, hot soak. There are towels in there and a clean bathrobe. I'll have something hot for you to drink when you come down." He closed the door behind him.

The saturated clothing made sucking sounds as Shaylee peeled them off. Michael's voice came through the door. "Hand me your wet things. I'll wring them out and throw them in the dryer."

A few moments later Shaylee opened the door a

crack and reached out one bare arm to shove a sodden mass into Michael's hands. Then she made a beeline for the deep, claw-footed tub, where the hot water soon brought her numbed fingers and toes back to life. Delicious warmth permeated her body as she lay in the bath, immersed up to her chin.

Half an hour later Shaylee descended, wrapped in an enormous white terry bathrobe that swept the floor behind her. She shuffled into the foyer, her hands lost inside the long sleeves which she kept trying to roll up. To her right was a roomy, cozy-looking kitchen, and on the center island waited two steaming glass mugs.

Across the hall in the living room, Michael was adding a log into the fireplace, where a crackling fire was blazing.

"Come sit by the fire and get cozy," he called.

Trying not to trip on the robe, Shaylee entered through the French doors. "What a lovely room," she exclaimed.

"Thanks. It's comfortable." Michael handed her a pair of wool socks. "Sorry I don't have slippers that'll fit you, but these'll keep your feet warm."

Shaylee pulled the socks on and grinned. "These aren't quite my size, either." Raising the hem of the robe, she did a little dance, making the toes of the socks flop in rhythm.

Michael chuckled. "You look like one of the Seven Dwarfs doing a tap dance."

Shaylee sank onto the cushions of the wine-coloured leather couch. Tucking her feet under her, she stretched her hands toward the fire.

"Still cold?" he asked. "I've fixed you a drink that should make you warmer." He went into the kitchen and returned with the glass mugs.

He handed her one and then raised his glass. "To your health."

Shaylee sipped the sweet beverage. A strong aroma of alcohol reached her nostrils. The taste wasn't unpleasant, but set her coughing. "Whew!" she coughed again. "What's in this?"

Michael seated himself beside her and she was very much aware of the arm he placed along the back of the couch behind her.

"Just some lemon, honey, hot water and brandy to get your blood circulating." He sipped his own drink. "Like it?"

"It does taste good. And it's certainly getting my blood circulating." After just a few swallows, a delicious heat began to flow through her.

She looked around. "I can see you've done a lot of work renovating this house, but I'm glad you left those old broad beams to crisscross the ceiling."

"Yes, I've made quite a few upgrades, especially in the kitchen. The plumbing and electricity were pretty antiquated. And of course I had to have a dishwasher installed."

Listening to him talk about the renovations, Shaylee drank the warm beverage quickly and set the empty mug on the table in front of her. Her head buzzed.

"Would you like another one?" Michael asked.

Her body glowed with waves of deliciously languid warmth. "Yes, thank you. That drink sure flushed any leftover ice out of my bones."

"That's what it was supposed to do." He went into the kitchen and soon returned with a refill. "I didn't put very much brandy in this time," he said. "You look pretty rosy and warm already."

Shaylee took a deep draft of her drink and then

began to untie the belt of the bathrobe. "Yes, I *am* getting kind of hot."

To her surprise, Michael quickly retied the belt. "I think it's best to leave that on. Maybe you could move away from the fire, if you're getting too warm."

He plucked the drink from her hand and placed it on the side table. "And maybe you don't even need the rest of this."

"Oh, no. I love this," Shaylee protested. She reached for the glass and took another big gulp. "And I love the fire. I love it. But these stockings are too, too much." She slipped her feet out of the wool socks and wiggled her bare toes.

Shaylee could see the smile on Michael's face and grinned back at him. He was such a nice guy. She sighed and leaned back on the couch while a languid feeling of satisfaction spread through her.

"This feels so-o delicious. You know, at home I go barefoot all summer and sometimes . . ." she lowered her voice to a whisper, "I get calluses on the bottoms of my feet. But I rub them all off with pumice stone. See?" She lifted her bare feet up for Michael's inspection. "No calluses."

For some reason Michael looked amused, which puzzled her. Calluses were a serious topic.

"No calluses," he observed and closed the bathrobe around her legs.

"Amazing stuff, pumice stone," Shaylee went on. For some reason her tongue felt thicker in her mouth and she found it difficult to speak. "You should try it if you have calluses somewhere. Have you got call-call-souses somewhere?" She took one of Michael's hands and felt the palm with her fingertips. "Nope, no calluses-es."

To Shaylee's bewilderment, Michael laughed. "Artists don't usually have calluses on their hands."

Shaylee brushed his palm lightly with her lips, and heard his sharp intake of breath. "Did you know lips are the most s-sensitive for feeling around with? Better than your fingers even, though fingers are s-s'posed to be there for feeling around with." She giggled at her own clever words and raised her hand up to his mouth. "S-see how s-sensitive your lips are?"

Michael gave each finger a quick, soft kiss. "You're right."

His gaze wandered to her mouth, making a delicious quiver ripple through her. "Would you like to s-see how s-sensitive my lips are? They're very s-sensitive, you know."

"Yes, I'm sure they are, but . . . but maybe not just now."

She looked at him with a concerned frown. "Your voice sounds kind of hoarse. Did you catch a cold?" She reached for her glass and finished her drink in one gulp.

He took the mug from her. "No, I don't think I did."

He felt so comfortably solid beside her. With a hiccup, she snuggled against him and smiled. "I liked the way you kissed my fingers. Kiss them some more. Please?"

Michael did, and Shaylee sighed. "I don't know how that feels to you, but it feels so nice to me. It tingles right up my arm." She closed her eyes as Michael's lips moved from her fingers to her wrist, where her pulse throbbed powerfully. She pulled up the sleeve of the robe to expose more of her arm to his lips. "I love the way your lips make me quiver all over."

The blood pounded in her ears. Waves of heat engulfed her, promising new, fiery thrills. She moaned softly and threw back her head.

"Kiss me here," she instructed, pointing to her throat, and when Michael obeyed, she moved her body in slow, languorous motions under his hands.

"Umm . . . nice. Very nice." She raised her arms which felt strangely heavy and languorous. She wrapped them around his neck and pulled him against her, tangling her fingers in his tawny hair. She wanted him closer. She wanted him . . .

Through the haze of yearning, Shaylee sensed Michael was no longer kissing her. She gave a little impatient whimper, but when he still didn't continue, she opened her eyes slowly and frowned.

"Why did you s-stop?"

"Shaylee." Michael's voice was a strangled whisper. "Shaylee, don't you know what's happening?"

Her eyes closed again and she gave a deep sigh. "No, but it's . . . nice," she mumbled.

She was asleep.

Michael covered her up with a light blanket and placed a pillow under her head before going into his room, away from this lovely little sleeping fairy.

From time to time he came to check in on her, as she slept on the couch, and each time he had an irresistible urge to brush aside a curl that threatened to disturb her sleep. And kiss her.

Thinking back to what had just transpired, Michael knew it had been a bad idea to sit so close to her. He should have used more self-control and removed himself to an armchair. But as Shaylee had pushed the terry robe out of the way and exposed her soft silky skin to him, he'd found it impossible not to continue planting delicious kisses up her arm. When the sleeve had prevented further advance, his lips had moved to the smooth roundness of her partly exposed shoulder. Then, on her invitation, he'd continued to the hollow at the base of her throat. With her warm, enticing cleavage only a kiss or two away, and with her moaning softly under him, he'd known he was getting too close to the precipice. It had been almost humanly impossible to stop himself from going over. But though he would have given a day of his life to continue, he knew he couldn't take advantage of her in her vulnerable state.

As Michael once again passed by the living room, which was dark except for the glow from the fireplace, he saw that Shaylee was awake. She was staring at the walls and ceiling where the light and shadows flickered in a playful dance and didn't seem to notice his presence. Did she even know where she was? Small wonder if she didn't, after gulping down that brandy so fast.

All at once she bolted up, as though suddenly becoming aware of her surroundings. But the next second she clutched her temples and slowly lay back down.

Michael winced. He honestly hadn't expected the drink to affect her so strongly, and he now had a pretty good idea of how she was feeling. Her head was probably pounding and he knew from experience there would be an unpleasant sensation in the pit of her stomach. Poor girl. He should have stopped her sooner, rather than indulge her wish to have more.

He was about to make her aware of his presence, but at that moment she rose, more slowly and cautiously this time, and clutching the robe around her weaved an unsteady path to the window. She pushed aside the curtain and looked out into the night. The full moon had risen. It cast sharp, black shadows of trees on the snow and made it glow with the brightness of daylight.

He coughed, and at the sound Shaylee started, but didn't turn around. Michael realized the last thing she wanted to do was to face him. He hesitated, hating to intrude, but then decided to face the inevitable and stepped into the room. Her stiff, straight back sure as hell didn't look welcoming.

"Good evening," he said as cheerily as he could under the circumstances. "Did you have a good nap?"

Her lack of response confirmed his suspicions. He tried to remain casual, and came to stand behind her, leaning one hand against the wall, while holding the curtain open wider with the other. "Beautiful, isn't it?" he murmured.

There was no response.

He had a strong urge to wrap his arms around her and hold her, but he wasn't about to do anything that stupid.

But then Shaylee turned her head to look up at him. Her eyes were bright in the moonlight and he tried to decipher the expression in them. Was this an invitation? Damned if it didn't look like one to him.

He took her by the shoulders and turned her slowly, drawing her near. She didn't resist, and seemed instead to mold herself against the length of him. The suppressed feelings from the afternoon, when he'd had to use all his willpower and determination to tear himself away from her, now returned like a storm. He brushed back her curls and held her face between his hands.

Her lips parted and Michael could no more stop

himself from kissing her than he could stop the moon from shining. Her mouth was soft and trembled under his. One hand holding her head, he pulled at the belt of the robe with the other. The wrap-around fell open, allowing his hand to slip inside and encircle her back. Her skin was smooth as satin under his palm and her body yielded to his touch. He tried to hold back, promising himself he would only taste the mind-numbing delight of her kiss, but the effort was futile.

A low growl rumbled in his throat. Once begun, he couldn't get enough of her. His kisses deepened and probed her eagerly responding mouth.

One hand moved to cup a small, firm breast and, as he caressed the aroused nipple, his other hand slipped lower, down her back to the velvety dip above her buttocks.

Suddenly Shaylee wrenched herself out of his arms. "No!" she cried, backing away. Her hands groped for the robe and then clutched it tightly around her. "How dare you," she hissed and her eyes flashed with angry sparks. "For the second time you're taking advantage of me, after bringing me here under the pretext of wanting to help."

Breathing heavily, Michael leaned against the wall, forcing himself to calm his turbulent emotions and hold himself in check. "I didn't take advantage of you this afternoon," he said as evenly as he could, "although it would've been easy enough to do."

Shaylee's voice was high-pitched with fury. "I'm sure it would have been, after getting me—" she stopped, her cheeks flushed crimson, "drunk with your powerful concoctions, so I didn't know which way was up."

"I only tried to get you warm. I honestly didn't think

you'd be affected like that." But Michael knew she wasn't listening to his useless protestations.

"You warmed me up, all right," Shaylee almost shouted. She turned and stomped out into the hall and up the stairs, the robe flowing behind her.

Michael swallowed down all attempts at defending himself. He knew any explanations would fall on deaf ears, but damned if he was going to let her think he was the only guilty party. She and the moon were at least partly to blame.

"I'm not sorry for this," he called after her.

Already halfway up the stairs, Shaylee stopped and whirled around. "I'll bet you're not," she spat out. "I'll bet from the moment I got into your car you planned this whole thing. Brought me here, gave me that drink, tried to seduce me in my . . . my condition."

But Michael didn't respond. His stony face staring up at her from the bottom of the staircase made Shaylee even more furious.

"This is all a game to you, isn't it?" Even as she lashed out, she knew she should stop right now, before she said something unforgivable. But she was too wound up to stop. "I honestly thought maybe, just *maybe*, you were the nice person you pretended to be when we were walking the other evening. What a sham that turned out to be. You were just trying to charm me into being another one of your . . . your groupies."

Michael's face registered surprise, but he remained quiet.

Her eyes filled, forming pools that threatened to spill out and flow down her cheeks. Which was something she didn't want him to witness.

"I hate you for spoiling the art classes for me!" she shouted, her voice trembling. She turned and ran up into the bedroom, slamming the door behind her with a wall-shuddering bang.

Wrapped in Michael's bathrobe, Shaylee stood trembling in the middle of the room, her breath coming out in agitated gasps. Then, to her dismay, she realized her clothes were still downstairs in the dryer. After yelling at him like that, how could she now go out and casually ask him to please get them for her.

Some time later she heard a firm knock on the door and went to open it, feeling totally sheepish. There stood Michael, holding a neatly folded stack of laundry.

"Your coat and boots aren't dry yet," he announced woodenly.

"Thank you," Shaylee replied in the same tone, took the clothes, and closed the door in his face.

Quickly she dressed, ran her fingers through her curls and went to the door. With her hand on the doorknob, she hesitated. Facing him, after everything that had happened, would be *very* awkward. Especially after her stormy accusations. Why couldn't she have bitten her tongue and remained silent and dignified, instead of shrieking like a fishwife? Oh, God! If only she hadn't drank all that brandy and made an embarrassing fool of herself. If only she could just erase this whole afternoon out of existence.

But she couldn't.

Well, what was done was done. She squared her shoulders and looked at herself in the full-length mirror to see if she could manage to look cool and dignified. She could, except for her shiny nose. She took a deep breath and opened the door. Then she proceeded to walk down the stairs, trying to retain as much of the cool and dignified look as possible.

She found Michael in the kitchen, grilling cheese sandwiches, judging from the aroma. The coffee brewing in the coffee maker smelled delicious and a sudden loud growl in her stomach reminded her she hadn't eaten since breakfast.

"I thought since you haven't had lunch or supper, the least I could do is make you a sandwich."

Shaylee detected a conciliatory note in his voice, but found the situation too uncomfortable and awkward to return the gesture. "No, thank you," she said, still trying to remain cool and dignified, although her mouth watered. "I have to go now. May I use your phone to call a cab?"

Well, she had to try, though his response was guaranteed to be negative.

"I'll take you home, but first you'll eat this sandwich." That was not a question and Shaylee knew better than to argue. Besides, she was too hungry to start debating with him.

"I ate while you were sleeping," Michael said, pushing the plate toward her.

Greedily she bit into the sandwich, while making a half-hearted effort to look reluctant. Then, without a shred of false modesty, Shaylee reached for the second sandwich, which also quickly disappeared.

After a mug of hot coffee, she felt much better. Amazing what a difference a full stomach and a steady head could make.

As soon as she'd finished, she asked that they leave and Michael didn't protest. He helped her into his jacket, since hers was still damp, and then held her arm while she slipped her feet into his huge black boots.

As she stood there waiting, suddenly Michael began

to chuckle.

Puzzled, Shaylee looked up at him. "What's so funny?" she asked, trying her best to sound annoyed.

"You look like—" He guffawed and turned her to face the full-length hall mirror. "Totally goofy."

Only her little nose and tousled hair were showing above the collar. His boots came up to her knees, where they met the hem of the jacket. She stood, looking at Michael who was cracking up.

Shaylee could no longer remain aloof. Soft giggles began to gurgle from inside her and soon she shook with a full-blown belly laugh. She laughed and laughed until her knees wobbled, while Michael was doubled over, clutching his stomach, looking fit to burst.

When they finally settled down, Shaylee found the laughter had washed away the last shreds of anger inside her. She reached for a tissue on the hall table and blew her nose.

"I don't know when I've laughed this hard," she said with a hiccup.

Michael nodded. "If laughter is the best medicine, then we both should be healthy for a pretty long while."

They stood looking at each other and the warm glow that lingered in the air was reflected on his face.

"Would you like to see my atelier?" he asked.

Chapter Seven

Before Michael realized what he'd said, the words were out and couldn't be taken back. A panicky feeling in the pit of his stomach told him he'd made a bad mistake. He wasn't ready to let her see his paintings. Why, in God's name, had he offered? What would she think of them? Of him? After having seen his work in the gallery, what would she say about the crap he had upstairs in his atelier? And he wasn't just thinking about the dirty coffee cups.

Too late. Before he could come up with a smart way to retract his words, Shaylee cried, "I'd love to! I've never seen a real atelier before. Only in movies."

Shaylee shed the boots and jacket and they climbed up to the studio on the third floor, while Michael's heart drummed a warning in his chest.

Shaylee hurried forward to inspect the room. Despite his anxiety, Michael couldn't help smiling at the way she walked around with a light step, looking around her with curiosity.

She turned to him, a delighted smile on her face. "It has a slanted roof and everything. Yes, it really is like the ateliers in the movies."

Paint tubes and containers of every size littered

most of the available counter space. There were dried paint splashes everywhere, and rags in all the hues of the rainbow hanging here and there like so many colourful banners. There were a couple of high bar stools, a dilapidated but cushy armchair, a few partly eaten donuts and, of course, the inevitable half-finished cups of coffee on the counter.

Brushes stood neatly in their holder and large sheets of paper were stacked on a wide shelf. Paintings in various stages of completion lay on tables, or hung by clips on the wires along the walls.

Eagerly Shaylee moved from painting to painting. But then her steps slowed and Michael saw her enthusiasm fade. Just as he'd feared would happen.

At last she turned to him, her forehead scrunched in puzzlement. "These are yours?"

The question hit him like an icy shower. Michael's heart slumped from his throat to his stomach, but he tried to pretend the question didn't hurt. "Who else would come to paint in my studio?"

"Hmm."

"What's that 'hmm' supposed to mean?" He forced out the question, though he knew damned well what it meant. She could tell something was wrong with the paintings.

"They're good but they're . . . they're not . . ."

Michael knew she was struggling to find words that would spare him the truth. His heart sank right down to his shoes, while a cold lump settled in his stomach.

He cleared his throat, and if there was any justice in the world his voice would not tremble. "What aren't they? What exactly are you trying to say?"

With almost masochistic cruelty he prodded her into saying what he would've given the world *not* to hear. He'd been making excuses long enough. It was time to stop fooling himself. He wanted her to say it straight to his face. No sparing his feelings.

As Shaylee raised her huge eyes to look directly into his, the freezing lump inside his gut grew into a glacier. He tried to force a rakish smile on his face but, damn it all, it was in danger of starting to wobble.

"Smack it to me, baby," he said lightly, hoping the pain didn't ooze through his words.

"Something's different," Shaylee finally choked out. "These aren't the same as the ones in the gallery."

Stupidly, he tried to make a joke of it. "Of course they're not the same. I don't paint with a stencil. Each painting's different."

She didn't even smile. "You know what I mean. There's something missing. I think they're . . ." she stopped, chewing her bottom lip. "They're nice and well done." She looked up at him earnestly. "But where's the depth and the sincerity I saw in the gallery? That's what they're lacking."

Michael gave up all silly pretenses. "Yeah, you're right," he said quietly. "I knew something just wasn't there, but I had to hear someone else say it."

And she was the someone he'd picked. Perhaps he had rashly invited her to come up because somehow, instinctively, he knew she would call it right. She wouldn't try to please him and say things she didn't mean. "Nice and well done. No depth or sincerity." God, she was exactly on the mark.

He snorted. "Good thing I never took them to show Max. He would've laughed me right out of the gallery," he said with a feeble attempt at bravado. "Thanks, little Fairy of the Field, you've done me a huge favour."

He had to turn away, averting her searching eyes.

Absently he picked up a tube of paint from the counter and squeezed it, twisting it out of shape. He wanted to reach out and hold someone . . . her, tightly against him to melt that scorching lump of ice inside him. But he knew she wouldn't want any part of him now that she knew the truth.

Nice? Well done? Damned if that wasn't the sort of stuff he said in class to encourage them along. But she wasn't saying it for encouragement. She was smacking him in the face with it. Telling it like it was.

Michael brushed a hand across his face to hide the moisture threatening to ooze out of his eyes. Max was right. He was washed up.

Just then there was a soft touch on his arm and he looked down at her hand resting there. The contact was barely palpable, but it burned through his clothing right into his frozen gut. Somehow it seemed to ease the pain.

"I'm sorry," Shaylee whispered. "I didn't mean to . . ." The tears shimmering on her lashes almost caused his own eyes to overflow.

To prevent a total meltdown, he shrugged and managed a shaky grin. "Hey, all artists go through a slump now and then." He patted her hand and missed it when it pulled away. "Someday, when you're a great artist, you'll see it's not going to be smooth sailing all the time. One day you'll wake up like me and realize you've lost your spark." He almost said soul but that would've sounded too heavy.

Shaylee could hear the quiver in his voice, despite his jocular attitude and the forced smile on his face. She knew he was trying to brush off the painful effect of her words, but was failing miserably. She wished she could have been gentler, or even have avoided telling him altogether. But, darn it all, something just wasn't right. His work lacked the passion—the soul—that had so strongly affected her in Max Storm's gallery. The wonderful quality that had inspired her to sign up for his classes simply wasn't evident here.

Why had his paintings changed? Or was it he who had changed?

Downcast, seeming almost embarrassed, Michael turned and picked up the water kettle.

"How about a cup of tea before I take you home?" he asked and plugged it in.

She could tell he was looking for an exit strategy, and her heart ached for him. She nodded and tried to avoid looking again at the paintings.

Silently they watched as the kettle began to hum and then bubbled. He gave her a teabag, poured boiling water into two paper cups, and handed her one. They were both pretending everything was normal, as they leaned their elbows on the counter and drank the hot tea.

Shaylee's fingers burned through the thin cardboard and she shifted the cup from hand to hand. "I think these cups are meant for cold drinks," she remarked. "Don't you have any mugs?"

He blew on his fingers. "And have to do a load of dishes? Uh-uh."

Shaylee laughed. "Two mugs do not a load of dishes make."

As she gingerly sipped the tea, her mind kept returning to the words Michael had spoken a moment ago. "Someday, when you're a great artist." He'd actually intimated this was a possibility for her. Despite the sadness she felt for him, she couldn't prevent her heart from giving a few joyful leaps.

"So you think *I* could actually be a great artist some day?" She threw the question out playfully, as though his answer didn't mean all the world to her.

"Why not?" Michael asked in turn. "If you have the talent, what you need is the will to learn, and the determination to succeed."

"It's very nice of you to say so." Nice. She'd actually used the word with total sincerity and not a trace of sarcasm. But although the answer should have made her feel hopeful, it left her with a niggling feeling of doubt. She had oodles of determination and certainly the will to learn, but he'd said "*if* you have the talent." Well, did she or didn't she? Darn it all, why couldn't he have been more specific?

She realized he'd shown his paintings to her even though he knew they weren't his best work, so wasn't it only fair that she should reciprocate and show him hers? But the mere thought made her throat constrict with fear and she knew she wasn't ready. Why did he have to keep her in the dark by making these vague comments? Why couldn't he tell her straight out she was talented?

Or not.

No, she wasn't ready to bring her painting to him.

Moments later, as they walked out to his car, Shaylee shuffled along in his boots, so they wouldn't fall off. Michael supported her by the arm so she wouldn't stumble.

"It would be simpler if I just carried you." he said.

Shaylee shook with giggles. "I can imagine what your neighbours would wonder. Is she ill? Is she drunk? Is she a new bride? And if she is, why is he carrying her out, instead of in?"

"And if she is, why is she wearing that huge jacket

instead of a bridal gown?" Michael added.

She got into the car with difficulty, the boots in danger of being left behind on the driveway. But finally, with a new attack of giggles, she managed to seat herself.

They sat in silence as Michael steered the car onto the street and headed north. Shaylee tried to decide which part of this very full and perplexing day she could comment on without bringing up anything unpleasant. Her freezing dunking, her drunkenness, her hissy fit, his paintings—there didn't seem to be too many pleasant topics available, so she remained silent. She refused to think about the kisses and the caresses that still made her skin tingle.

But after a while Michael coughed, hesitated, and then blurted out, "I want to tell you I'm truly sorry I made you angry with my behavior today."

This was exactly the subject Shaylee wanted to avoid. "Michael, please don't. I was the clumsy fool who fell into the river. You were very heroic in rescuing me and taking me to your home to warm me up, and . . ." She didn't want to mention her fit of anger, but now that the gate was open, she decided to press on. "I want to apologize for the way I shouted at you, after all your kindness. Please forgive me. Honestly, I don't know what got into me."

"It's obvious I crossed a line and that made you very uncomfortable. And you weren't exactly yourself, either."

Shaylee nodded. "Yes." Her heart raced at the memory. It was no use denying she'd *wanted* Michael to do exactly what he'd done. And to keep on doing it. Which was probably why she'd been so angry . . . at herself.

"Believe me, I brought you to my place with the

most chivalrous of intentions," he continued. "The drink was supposed to warm you up, I mean de-ice you, not get you all hot, like . . . uh." He stopped and grinned sheepishly. "Like the way it did."

Shaylee groaned. "Please. Let's not talk about it."

But he went on. "It's just that sitting there, kissing my hand, you were so enticing."

Horrified, she turned to face him. "I was not kissing your hand."

"Well, you were touching it with your lips, and to me that's kissing. And I'm afraid the effect it had on me was . . . well, you can probably imagine."

Shaylee imagined, and luckily the darkness hid her face.

"I didn't mean to get so carried away," Michael said, "but when you . . ."

Shaylee cringed. "Please, spare me the details."

"Look, I hope you understand you were very desirable and I had to do some pretty stern talking to myself to get me to stop, especially when you were begging me to continue."

"I did *not* beg!" But yes, in fact she'd been doing exactly that. And suddenly, the delicious fires that had throbbed through her in the afternoon returned and left her breathless. Good thing Michael was negotiating a left turn at the lights and didn't see how her cheeks were burning.

Michael stopped at a red light and turned to Shaylee. "Please believe that I'm a good guy at heart. I didn't have any nefarious intentions when I brought you home. Things just kind of evolved."

Was she listening? Did she believe him? As the light turned green, he stepped on the gas and the passing streetlights intermittently illuminated the interior of the car. She sat beside him, almost drowning inside his big coat. He wanted to stop the car and kiss her. "I'll never forgive myself if you stop coming to the art classes. I don't want to lose you."

Lose her? Something squeezed his heart. Was he losing his grip on reality?

"Lose you as a student," he quickly amended. "Even if sometimes you're a bit stubborn and contrary."

"What?" she squeaked. "Stubborn? *Moi*?"

Michael pulled up at the curb in front of her apartment building and came around to help her as she struggled with the big boots. In the front foyer they both eyed the staircase.

"Too bad there's no elevator in this building," she said. "This is going to be very difficult and extremely comical."

"Look, I meant what I said earlier about carrying you," he said and, without another word, he whisked her into his arms. He took the stairs two at a time up to the third floor, not at all impeded by the heavy boots and bulky jacket.

Shaylee laughed. "I always liked the part in *Gone with the Wind* where Clark Gable carries Scarlet O'Hara up that wide staircase."

"But lucky Clark didn't have to deposit her at the door," Michael said as he set her on the hall floor. "He got to—"

"So, thank you for helping me," Shaylee cut in hastily. "Yet another chivalrous deed you can add to today's list."

Thinking back to everything that had happened today—everything that had almost happened—he would have given anything to carry her into the apartment like Clark Gable. The thought of what had ensued in the movie gave his heart a jolt.

Hampered by the long sleeves, she fumbled with the key and dropped it on the hall floor.

"Oh, drat."

"Here, let me." Michael picked up the key and opened the door for her. Then, before she could slip inside, he took hold of her shoulders and made her look directly at him. "So, I'll see you Monday night?"

But she ducked out of his hands and called over her shoulder, "I'll bring your coat and boots to class. Good night. And thanks again."

Although she shut the door in his face, he grinned. If he hadn't been wearing heavy winter shoes, he would have jumped up and clicked his heels.

She was coming back.

Michael's steps echoed in the stairwell as he slowly descended, deep in thought. Why did he feel this elated simply because a student hadn't quit? Because her work intrigued and excited him. That's why. And because she was able to breathe life into the most mundane practice piece. Beside her paintings, the other students' work looked lifeless and stilted.

Like his own present efforts looked beside his past ones. But why had his work changed? In his youth his creativity had soared and he'd never had this problem. So what happened? Sure, the ugly fights with Ashley had made him cynical, but was that why he'd lost his spark? Surely not.

Michael emerged out onto the street, swung open his car door, and got in. But instead of pushing the start button he sat staring into the wintry night. A light came on in a window on the third floor and a slender shadow appeared against the drawn blind. His mind shot back a couple of hours to when he held her in his arms. The full moon. The shadows. Her silky smooth skin. . .

Enough! He was straying into forbidden territory.

From now on he would have to guard his moves with her, or he stood a chance of losing her . . . as a student, of course. But it wouldn't be easy, not after today. A feeling of loss crept into his heart because he knew he would have to deny himself something wonderful he had only discovered. Like some exquisite wine, she was going to his head, making him want more. More of what he knew he must not have.

The clock in the Queen's Park tower rang twelve times as Michael stepped out from the downtown office tower and immediately he shucked off his jacket. Conferring all morning with a client, he hadn't realized the day had turned so warm and sunny. When had spring arrived? It seemed only yesterday he'd seen kids trudge to school past his house in bulky jackets and heavy boots, and here he was today, basking in the glorious warmth of the noontime sun. As he strolled toward his car parked at a curbside meter, he rolled up his shirtsleeves to catch every welcome ray on his sun-starved skin.

But he hadn't walked more than a few steps among the swarming lunch-hour crowd, when he saw a familiar figure standing on the street corner, waiting for the light to turn. Shaylee! After recovering from the unexpected, but pleasant surprise, he hurried over and lightly touched her shoulder.

She twirled around with a start, but when she recognized him, her face broke into a wide, happy smile. Her curls fringed her face like a sunny halo and the off-white blouse and slim navy skirt complimented her trim figure.

"What is little Fairy Princess of the Field doing here in the middle of a crowded business section of Toronto?" Michael asked.

She laughed. "I'm making a living as my alter-ego, 'Shaylee the Assistant Manager'. Even us wee folk has gotta eat."

"I thought you only ate nectar and dew and stuff like that."

She certainly looked as if she would do just that. Was it her elfin eyebrows that gave her this fairy look? Once again his imagination dressed her in a gauzy, transparent gown with shimmering fairy-wings on her back. How he wished he could paint her, right after first kissing that delicious mouth of hers. It would bring a delicate blush to those cheeks and—

A throaty laugh nudged him back to reality. "Only in the summer," his Fairy said. "Every winter we wood-folk come to the city to eat pizza. But what're you doing here?"

"Visiting a client," he replied. "I'm doing a mural for his office lobby. You had lunch yet?"

"No, I just came out." Shaylee spread her arms, as if to gather the sunshine to her breast. "I simply could-n't sit in the cafeteria."

"I'd like to take you for lunch, but I must admit I don't know any decent dew and nectar joints around here. Would a deli sandwich do?"

Her delighted laughter made him feel warm inside. "It would. Thanks."

A short time later they were seated on a park bench with their take-out sandwiches, near the statue of some Very Important Royalty on horseback. Not far away, Queen Victoria looked sternly down her nose at them from her throne. A variety of other stony faces envied their simple meal. The lawn around them was pristine green, except for a few dandelions that had managed to sneak by the city gardeners.

"I like dandelions," Shaylee said wistfully, gazing at a bright yellow flower near them. "Especially first thing in the spring."

Yeah, he figured she would. She was a dandelion kind of girl.

"My grandpa always said," she went on, "if there were only a few dandelions in the world, they'd be gracing everyone's buffet table. Too bad they're so abundant nobody wants them."

"Except kids. I remember my kindergarten teacher had a special little vase on her desk for all those stem-less dandelion blossoms we brought her." Michael grinned at the memory. "My bouquet—and I use the word loosely—was in that vase once, and I still remember how proud I was."

Shaylee tried to imagine how he'd looked as a five-year old. Endearingly cute, for sure, with his dancing brown eyes. It made her want to know everything about him. His childhood, his teen years, his dreams for the future. But it wasn't likely they would ever be close enough for such intimacies.

"I bet you were a really cute kid," Michael said, mirroring her thoughts.

Cute? For most of her life she'd resented being tagged with that word, but somehow she liked the way he said it. It didn't sound condescending.

"I guess it won't come as a surprise if I say I was pretty small," she mused, then asked, "So how come you aren't married with kids and all that?" She hoped her voice didn't sound like she was fishing for information. Which, of course, she was. Nonchalantly she sipped coffee from the paper cup.

Michael took a bite of his deli sandwich, and wiped a spot of mustard off his chin with his thumb. He seemed to be weighing his response and Shaylee was sorry she'd asked.

"I was married once," he said at last. "But my wife saw me for what I am and left."

"What do you mean she saw you for what you are?" The question popped out before she had time to consider its appropriateness.

Michael didn't seem to mind. "I'm pretty selfish, you know. I didn't realize how much I'm consumed by my art until Ashley brought it to my attention in a rather shrill manner." He gave a short, dry laugh. "Things between us had been sliding into a mud hole for some time, so it didn't come as a surprise when she announced she'd had enough of me and my art, and left. She wanted to have kids, like most women do, I guess."

His voice took on a hard, almost defiant tone. "But that didn't fit into my life style, and that fact hasn't changed. I can't see how I could give a woman what she wants and be free to live my life the way *I* want." He released a long sigh. "It feels great to be able to paint without feeling guilty."

"But you must have loved her, though."

Michael didn't answer for so long that Shaylee's lunch began to churn unpleasantly in her stomach. Was he still hurting about the breakup?

"I guess," he said at last. Slowly he crumpled his sandwich paper, as though he were thus eradicating the existence of the relationship. "Probably I did, or why would I have married her, eh?"

Shaylee didn't want to intrude into his thoughts again, much as she wanted to find out more.

After another long silence he continued. "This may sound stupid and juvenile, but even at my age I don't think I know what love's supposed to feel like." His eyes looked directly into hers. "Do you?"

Shaylee lowered her lids, afraid of what her eyes might reveal. She plucked a blade of grass beside her before replying quietly. "I'm counting on the fact that when I fall in love—I mean, *truly* fall in love—I'll know. I hope so, anyway."

Michael nodded. "Maybe. Art has always been my number one love and I have to be selfish about it so I can do what I feel I'm meant to do with my life. So a selfish person like me better not get into any permanent relationships. It would be totally unfair of me to ask a woman to play second fiddle to my art. No self-respecting woman would agree to that, anyway."

Shaylee didn't like the picture he painted of himself. "I'm sure you're not half as selfish as you're making yourself out to be. If you were, you couldn't paint like you do." She paused, then spoke quietly to her coffee cup. "Like you did. Like your work in the gallery."

The silence that followed her words was almost palpable and told her he didn't want to go in this direction. Why had she brought it up, anyway?

"Ashley's married now," Michael continued abruptly, disregarding her words. "And she has the baby she wanted. She juggles her career, a very fashionable home and her family with great dexterity. A very successful woman, I must admit. And happy, too, as far as I know."

"And you?" Shaylee asked looking up.

Michael dimpled a playful smile at her. "Am I successful? Naturally. As for happy . . ." The smile became slightly strained. "I'm totally content. I have my freedom, which is absolutely essential to me, so I can put all my energy into my art. I don't want a heavy anchor in my life." He threw his scrunched paper bag at a nearby wire wastebasket and missed.

"Oh, I see. Is that why you carry on in class with—" Shaylee put the brakes on, but not before Michael had caught on.

"With the women?" He sounded more amused than insulted.

Hastily, Shaylee tried to back-pedal. "I'm sorry. It's none of my business. I should not have said that."

"My little country girl disapproves? I *thought* I detected a censoring look in your eyes that first night in class."

His teasing grin annoyed her. "First of all," she snapped, "I'm not your little anything. And secondly, I just have different views on those things." She raised her chin haughtily. "To which I am entitled."

Her outburst sobered him and his eyes lost their mischievous glint. "I'm sorry. I didn't mean to offend."

"That's all right." Shaylee smoothed out the sandwich wrapper on her knee. "I shouldn't be spouting off about things that don't concern me."

"So what exactly *are* your views on those things?"

Although she found it difficult, she looked into his eyes. "Well, since you asked. I don't believe in bed-hopping."

"It's only a diversion, that's all. Taking care of my needs, so to speak."

"I don't care for diversions of that sort. In my view sex is not for entertainment. It's a sign of commitment. And there's no commitment in one-night stands."

"Precisely. And that's why they're so good for some-one in my situation. No commitment. For you, of course, there has to be marriage before sex." Again he sounded like he was teasing her.

"Not necessarily," she replied, thinking of Steve back home. "I understand my views don't apply to everyone, but I believe whether it's sex before or after marriage, it's important that there be a strong emo-tional attachment. Otherwise it's just a shallow game."

Clouds were gathering in the west, threatening to cast a shadow over the sunny day. With a sigh, Shaylee crumpled up her sandwich paper and stuffed it into a paper bag. Their happy conversation was threatening to turn into a confrontation.

"Well, games are fine for me," he declared. "I have places to go and things to do." He rose with a stretch and went to pick up his sandwich paper, which he de-posited into the basket with an exaggerated gesture.

"So are you planning any trips at the moment?" she asked, striving for a casual tone. She didn't really care. She was just curious.

"Yes, as a matter of fact I'm going to Europe for a year," he replied. His eyes lit up with enthusiasm that failed to ignite the same response in her.

"A year?" Having just eaten, Shaylee couldn't un-derstand why she suddenly felt so empty. She wanted him to stay, because . . . because she wanted him as her teacher. And her friend. Being with him was not only enlightening, but also pleasant. "And who's going to look after your business? And the art lessons?"

"My associates will carry on with our clients and they'll run the art classes," Michael explained. "Mika, Miguel, and I take turns going off for a year to study and paint. In fact, Mika Laine's in Africa right now, getting 'rejuvenated' as we call it. It's too easy to fall into a slump." He stopped.

Slump. Shaylee looked at her hands, so he wouldn't know she'd seen the flash of embarrassment in his eyes.

As though confirming her thoughts, he went on, "I think that's probably what's happened to me. I've fallen into a slump. So I'm looking forward to my rejuvenating year abroad. I think it'll get me back on track."

"Yes, I'm sure it will," she agreed, not wanting to pursue the subject that made him uncomfortable. But in her mind she was starting to connect the dots. Did the fact he'd shut love out of his life explain the lack of soul in his work? Maybe. But what did she know about those things?

Rising, she threw her balled-up paper bag into the wastebasket. "Bulls eye!" she exclaimed victoriously.

"Nice of you to show me off," Michael grumbled. They started to cross the lawn, back toward the office buildings.

"So where will you be going to rejuvenate yourself?" she asked.

"I'm going to Paris and Rome and other centers of art in Europe. I've contracted to give some lectures on Canadian art at a few art colleges, and naturally I'll be doing the usual tourist stuff." He seemed to come alive as he spoke. "But mainly I want to get fresh ideas by studying art history, going to galleries and interacting with other artists."

His excitement stirred a sense of adventure in her. Maybe he was right and going to Europe was exactly what he needed. "So when do you leave?" she asked.

"I've booked a passage on a cruise ship leaving New

York in the fall," he told her. "Want to come along?"

"Yes, of course I'll come," she replied with gaiety she didn't feel. "Oh, wait. I only get two weeks off for holidays. Sorry, no can go."

"Too bad."

"But, wow! A cruise ship? I'm green with envy." Though envy wasn't exactly what she was feeling. It was more like the sadness of one who was left behind on the shore, watching the ship depart.

They came to a busy intersection and Michael put out his hand for her. She slipped hers into it and, like in that first class, her hand felt like it belonged there. They crossed the street, and the warmth from his hand radiated into her. Did he feel it, too?

"Yes, I'm looking forward to the trip," he went on. "People ask why I don't save time by flying, but I wouldn't want to miss the opportunity of experiencing the ocean in its many moods. Each time I cross, I see something new."

"Each time you cross? And here's me who's never been in anything bigger than a bathtub." She wanted him to keep holding her hand. It felt good, like he cared. Which he didn't, of course. But, still . . .

"Really?"

"Okay. So I'm lying." She laughed ruefully. "I *have* made the crossing to Toronto Island on the ferry."

Michael grinned. "Practically an old saltie then."

They stopped in front of the office building where Shaylee worked. Their moment together had to end, but she was reluctant to pull her hand away. All at once Shaylee heard the clock in the Queen's Park tower ring the half hour and she gasped. "Oh, my goodness. Look at the time. I'm half an hour late."

"It's my fault. I was enjoying myself so much, I didn't even think of checking the time." Michael released her hand and pushed open the wide glass door for her. They entered the bright, spacious lobby with its shiny marble floor and high glass ceiling with chandeliers.

Shaylee pressed an elevator button. "No, I should have checked. It's my lunch hour. You artists aren't tied to clocks and things." Nor to people.

"Or so we'd like to believe. But when there's a business to run, I'm afraid there are a few nasty restrictions and deadlines. But you're right. Generally I come and go as I please."

The elevator doors opened and a group of people in dark business suits filed out. Michael put a hand on her shoulder and smiled. "Thanks for a great lunch. I'll see you tonight?"

Shaylee slipped into the elevator. "Marita and I'll be there," she said as the doors closed and shut him from view.

Chapter Eight

Michael dabbed a couple of strokes on the painting he was working on and then stepped back to take a look. Not bad. It was amazing how nowadays the old joy of painting had him jumping out of bed each morning, ready to work on his projects. He hadn't felt this stimulated for so long, it was totally electrifying. Each day he wanted to get as much done as possible before some constraint or other forced him out of his atelier.

Like now, he had to get to class. Pronto. But he didn't resent it, because Shaylee would be there. No use trying to deny this. It took all his willpower to stop thinking about her every moment he was away from her. She was like a song that refused to leave his brain, and he always looked forward to seeing her. As well as seeing the work she produced each week in class. He rinsed out his brush, placed it in a jar with others, and after giving his work an approving nod, he hurried downstairs.

As Michael stepped out the door he came to a sudden halt. How had he failed to notice that the golden forsythia bushes by the southern wall were already in bloom? Almost every spring, their sudden flush of colour caught him by surprise. He grinned. The sneaky little devils.

When he parked on the street by the fruit market, masses of flowers in buckets of water overflowed from the store onto the sidewalk. A riot of colours—red tulips, purple hyacinths, bright yellow daffodils, blue irises—almost assaulted his eyes. He bought a dozen daffodils and then strode up the stairs to the studio. Trying to capture the delicate beauty of the blossoms on paper would be a good exercise for the students.

As Michael distributed a few daffodil stems on every table, his mind kept circling back to Shaylee. Why this strange obsession with her? If he didn't know any better, he would have said he was falling for her. If some guy had described to him the same symptoms that roiled inside him, Michael would've laughed and said the guy was obviously a goner—hook, line, and sinker. But that couldn't be happening to *him*. A person couldn't fall in love if he absolutely did *not* want to.

Or could he?

They'd met a few times for lunch downtown and each time they'd had fun. Sure, it had taken some serious juggling on his part to arrange the meetings, but he was okay with that. He cherished these outings with her. Perhaps a tad too much. Frustrated, Michael ran his fingers through his hair. Time to get his horses back into the stable.

To his relief people started arriving for class, so he couldn't think about this any more.

Shaylee got right to work, enthusiastic about painting the daffodils. She loved flowers and they'd often been her subject of choice back home.

When Marita turned to look at Shaylee's work a while later, she gave a low whistle. "Bingo! You've got them right on," she breathed. "I could pluck them off the paper and put them in a vase."

"Thanks. I guess I do paint flowers pretty well," Shaylee conceded, trying not to sound vain. It was difficult to remain modest because the flowers did look very real.

Marita studied her own painting. "Somehow, mine look like yellow tin cans balancing on green sticks."

"With ruffled doilies around them," Shaylee added helpfully.

"Yes, that too," Marita agreed. "But they were *supposed* to be daffodils."

"That's true. They were."

"But I guess I could say I actually *meant* to paint yellow tin cans, couldn't I?" Marita chewed the end of her brush thoughtfully.

Marita's deadpan humour made Shaylee giggle. "Of course. It's your painting."

"But you *could* tell me they look nice."

"Well, since you're groveling . . . all right. They're very pretty yellow tin cans on lovely green sticks. There, is that better?"

"And I do like those ruffled doilies," Michael said, coming up behind them. Obviously he'd overheard.

Marita tapped him on the arm with her brush. "You, sir, are not kind."

"I agree, he is definitely not kind," Britney chimed from across the room.

Shaylee frowned. Who invited her into the conversation?

"How'm I not kind?" Michael asked, turning to look at Britney.

"You're not kind, because last week I left a message on your phone asking you to come over and you didn't even return my call," Britney thrust out her full lower lip in a pout.

Michael shrugged unapologetically. "Sorry. I've been busy."

Britney raised her brush with a smooth, exaggerated flourish, ensuring everyone's attention was focused on her. With almost hypnotic smoothness she asked, "Have you, dear?"

Michael strode to Britney's table with measured steps. "What's on your mind?"

Shaylee could hear her audible, purring reply. "Busy with little Field Fairies, perhaps?"

He didn't respond, only glanced at Britney's painting over her shoulder.

"That daffodil leaf," Michael said, pointedly, "reminds me of a dagger. Could you try for a bit more delicacy?"

She placed a hand on his arm, but Shaylee was pleased to see him shrug it off and move on to the next table to look at Bruce's work. Or was it Burt's?

Helena's fretful voice rang from across the room. "Please, Michael, do come quickly. My daffodil is turning into an awful mess. Can you do something to revive it?"

Michael walked over to examine the painting. "It seems you've rubbed that part out so many times the surface of the paper is wearing thin. I'm afraid there's nothing I can do, but console you for the loss of your flower."

Helena's burst of throaty laughter rang out in the silent room. "Oh, Michael, it's a bit late for that, isn't it?"

Shaylee sat, chewing her bottom lip, and tried not to listen.

It seemed the class was waiting for Michael's reaction, but he refused to grace the indelicate remark with a reply.

"Everyone, come on up," he said calmly. "I'll show you how to shade the long, bent daffodil leaves."

As Shaylee walked with Marita to Michael's table, she could hardly contain her anger at Britney and Helena. But at the same time she was pleased with the way Michael had brushed off their vulgar comments. In fact, Shaylee had noticed that in the last week or two he'd rarely responded to their flirtations. Marita had even stopped calling him Lothario.

Yes, she was definitely growing too fond of him. Each time they met downtown on her lunch hour, this feeling grew stronger. She would have liked nothing better than to allow their friendship to develop into something closer, but she knew that was not wise. The leopard might have changed his spots, but his philosophy was still the same. No permanent relationships for him.

They never alluded to the evening at his house. Probably he'd forgotten all about it. After all, it had only been a simple kiss, and for a man like Michael, what was there to remember? But Shaylee relived it over and over again, as she lay in the darkness on her lonely bed.

Her mind preoccupied, she found it difficult to concentrate on the demonstration lesson. Lately Michael hadn't made any negative comments about her work. Not that he'd said anything that sounded remotely like praise, either, but maybe soon it would be time to bring her painting from home and get his opinion on it.

When she returned to work at her table, Shaylee tried to think about nothing but long, bent daffodil leaves. She was happy with the clear hues she'd produced on the flowers, and the straight stems and leaves received more lavish praises from Marita. She was satisfied with her painting and dared to hope that maybe tonight Michael would, at last, say she had talent. And then she would bring him the painting that awaited at home, and—

"If you understood what I was demonstrating in my lesson, you'll see your leaves need clearer outlines." Michael had come up behind her and bent over to see her work.

Crunch! Here she'd been congratulating herself, and he came along to find fault with her work. Was it possible to *ever* get him to say "Bravo"?

Shaylee swallowed down her anger. "I kind of like them the way they are." She tried not to sound like a pouting kid. "I don't want them to look like outlined cartoons."

She could feel Michael's fingers tense up on the back of her chair, the knuckles hard against her shoulder blade.

"I wasn't talking about cartoons, and you know it," he said evenly. "I suggested clearer outlines, which you can achieve with shading."

"But if I outline them, they *will* look like cartoons," she insisted.

He picked up her paint board and inspected the daffodils closely.

Darn it all, he *had* to see that the flowers were a delicate, almost transparent yellow. And she'd tried so hard to infuse the stems and leaves with that stiff quality, unique to daffodils. Was the man blind not to see that?

Shaylee looked up at him. "I hope you notice that I

tried to make the leaves kind of unyielding, like daffodils tend to be, you know? Sort of stubborn." She
hoped her voice was conciliatory, but obviously it was-
n't. She could tell his jaw was clenched in anger when
he put the painting down.

"Unyielding and stubborn? Like the painter herself,"
he muttered. "The object of today's lesson was how to
use shading to emphasize details, and I suggest you
try to do that."

His words sounded harsh and commanding. Shades
of old Mr. Crawley.

"Personally, I like the way it looks. I paint delicately." She tried to keep her voice quiet and flat so he
wouldn't see how furious she was growing.

"Yes, you do. But part of learning is trying different
techniques to see how they work. However, if you think
you know better, then perhaps you should take over
the class."

He was probably trying to make his words sound
like a joke, but his stiff, hard-lipped smile told her
something different.

Shaylee responded with a similar, insincere grimace. "If I were the teacher, I'd let my students be creative and not criticize their every effort."

"Everyone has to start from somewhere, my dear.
People can't create from nothing. Even your former
teacher, Leonardo da Vinci, learned from the past
masters. Remember?" Michael turned and marched to
the other end of the room. Shaylee saw his dark brows
knit together as he leaned over to look at Pauline's
work.

"Boy! Doesn't he sound just like Mr. Crawley,"
Shaylee muttered to Marita. "Where in the world did
they both learn the words to that same old song about

past masters? I only want to paint like me, and not do everything like he says."

"You *do* paint like you. And in my humble opinion, which is never taken seriously, you paint better than anyone in this room." The whispered words were for Shaylee's ears alone.

"Well . . ." Shaylee tried not to look smug, although she had to agree. "If I do, why doesn't he say anything good about my work?" she whispered back. "I don't hear him say anything negative to Bruce or Burt. Or criticize anyone else's efforts. He simply doesn't like *anything* I do."

"Michael only asked you to try what he had shown in his demonstration lesson. That's fair enough, in my opinion."

"Well, he *never* thinks my work is satisfactory. He's always telling me to do this and change that." Shaylee's chin jutted out stubbornly. Although she knew she sounded like an irascible little brat, she was too angry to care. She'd hoped so hard tonight would finally be *the* night, but again she found her dreams in tatters.

Marita continued to dab yellow paint on her tin cans. "The way I see it, Michael doesn't bother to criticize the rest of us, because he doesn't want to expend his energies trying to make silk purses out of sows' ears. You, however, are worth teaching and guiding along."

The words made Shaylee feel like a silly, rebellious teenager. Embarrassed, she kept her gaze on her painting.

Marita gave her a sidelong glance. "Besides, from what I understood, that's what you wanted him to do, wasn't it? Tell you if it's good or not?"

"Mmm." Shaylee shrugged uncomfortably. Actually she only wanted him to tell her it was *good*. But she couldn't very well say so to her friend. "I guess I owe him an apology," she muttered at last.

Marita nodded. "Uh-huh."

With hesitant steps, Shaylee walked to the other end of the room where Michael was helping Tracy. The water taps were in that direction so she took her dish along as an excuse to go near him.

"Michael," she said tentatively, addressing his back, hoping he wouldn't spurn her peace offering. "When you have a moment, could you come over to my table?"

Michael's head came up, a look of surprise in his eyes. "Sure," he said. "I'll be there in a minute."

As soon as he arrived, Shaylee blurted out, "I'm sorry for balking at your suggestion." She spoke quietly so the rest of the room wouldn't stop breathing to listen. "There was no excuse for it."

Michael smiled his forgiveness. "It's okay. At least you have opinions and ideas of your own." His hand came to rest on her shoulder.

And burned right through her old t-shirt. He *had* to feel the way she tensed under it. "I tried the shading and outlining, and actually it doesn't look half-bad," she confessed and shyly held out her paint board for him to see. "I guess I shouldn't be afraid to use stronger colours."

"Looks good."

"Thanks." Shaylee could tell his words were sincere, and she appreciated that.

As she and Marita walked slowly home in the soft spring night, the heady awakening spring scents surrounded them. Shaylee pulled a twig off a bush by the sidewalk and smelled the freshly unfurled, sticky leaves. Things were ever so much more pleasant now that peace reigned between her and Michael again.

"I'm glad my silly behavior tonight didn't affect my relationship with Michael."

Marita spun to face Shaylee. "Your relationship?" she enthused. "Boy, I'm all for that."

"I'm talking teacher-student relationship," Shaylee clarified. "I love coming to classes. I'll be sad when they're over." She felt a tug in her heart that said the classes wouldn't be the only thing she'd be missing. Soon Michael would be gone out of her life forever.

"Sad? That's a unique way of putting it," Marita said. "I'll certainly miss the classes, too, but I can't honestly say I'll be *sad*."

Shaylee raised her chin. "That's because I'm very serious about my art." She knew her explanation didn't make any sense, but Marita seemed to accept it. "I'm totally determined someday I'm going to reach my goal."

Tonight Michael had said her painting looked good. Maybe she shouldn't be so happy about such meager crumbs, but she was. "I can taste success," Shaylee declared. She threw her arms open wide to embrace all of Toronto and the surrounding suburbs as well.

"Yes, I understand your hunger," Marita agreed. "But is that any reason to feel sad about the end of the lessons?"

"Yes. Because Michael shouldn't go gallivanting off to Europe when I need him." She needed him to tell her she was fabulous. She needed him because—

"I know. But *sad*?"

"Sad, sad, sad," Shaylee snapped. "Your needle's stuck in a groove, Marita." She knew what her friend was fishing for, but she wasn't about to 'fess up to anything. "There's no other relationship, if that's what you're trying to sniff out. I just like to talk with him."

"Yes?"

"About *art.*"

She had to admit she always looked forward to their chance meetings downtown, and couldn't help being disappointed if he wasn't waiting for her in the lobby. They'd go for a quick lunch at a nearby cafe and talk. Mainly about art, but also about everything and nothing. Yes, she was definitely getting too fond of him and it would be hard not to see him any more.

They walked on in the darkness, stopping now and then to take in the aroma of dewy lilacs that seemed to grow in almost every yard they passed.

Out of the blue Marita asked, "So why don't you go to Europe with him? You told me he asked you."

"Marita, I told you he was *joking,*" Shaylee blustered. "He's never asked me seriously. You're being ridiculous."

"Well, if he asked you seriously, would you go?"

Something about Marita reminded her of a terrier. The woman never let go of an idea if she thought it had an ounce of merit. This idea, however, had less than none.

"All right, I'll come clean," Shaylee said with a huge sigh. "I wouldn't mind going to Europe to study and paint. I mean, what artist in her right mind wouldn't? But I wouldn't want to go with *Michael.*" Yes, she did, but she never would.

"Why not? You two could have a beautiful rela—"

"Marita!" Shaylee almost shrieked into the night. "Get real." She lowered her voice as they passed a couple out for an evening walk. "I've told you he doesn't want permanent relationships in his life. And I don't want to go as some mistress, or whatever, and then be dumped when we returned to Canada."

"Whoa, I didn't say anything about being his mistress, did I? What's wrong with a friendly relationship? Partners. Platonic-like."

"Platonic-like?" Shaylee's voice rose to a squeak. "With a guy like Michael? Pardon me if I chuckle."

As if that were possible. The kisses they'd shared, about which her friend knew nothing, were proof something could easily develop between them if she let down her guard. She knew Michael had no compunction about striking up a purely physical relationship at the drop of a hat. But not she. As she'd said to him, there had to be a strong emotional tie before sex, which certainly was lacking on his part. As for her, she was afraid her heart was not obeying her very well right now.

"Okay. I get it," Marita conceded. "It was a silly idea."

"Yes, it was."

Shaylee's sharp reply put an end to the conversation. Or maybe Marita let up because they'd reached their apartment building. She held open the door for Shaylee. "Talent before beauty," she said, bowing.

"Thank you." Head held high, Shaylee floated past Marita and they began to trudge up the stairs. "I know I should try to believe what you said about sows' ears and silk purses, and not get so offended every time he criticizes my work. But I wish for *once* he'd simply come out and say, 'Shaylee, you're great.' Then I could stop doubting myself."

They reached the third floor and Marita sighed heavily as she continued up one more floor. "What you have to do is show Michael that painting on your wall," she called down the stairwell. "His 'Wow!' will make your doubts evaporate. But for heaven's sake, don't take *my* word for it! After all, what do *I* know?"

Triple M Graphic Design and Production was located downtown on the main floor of one of the many century homes that had been converted into office space. While Mika Laine was slowly making his way home from Africa, where he'd been studying and teaching for the past year, Michael and Miguel Cordova kept the business running.

Michael entered the office on Tuesday morning much earlier than usual and slammed the door shut behind him. Sleep last night had been impossible, so he'd got up and headed for work, instead of trying to coax another hour of shut-eye from his wide-awake brain.

What a damned mess everything was. And he wasn't thinking about the state in which he'd left the studio last night, either. Shaylee was the cause of it all. The woman had somehow snuck under his skin and wormed her way deep inside him. She had spunk. And talent. Not to mention beauty and sincerity.

Snagging his jacket on a hook by the door, Michael went into the alcove that served as a small kitchenette, and set up the coffeemaker. He drummed his fingers on the counter as he waited for the perking to finish. On top of all that, Shaylee seemed to provide him with the one ingredient absolutely vital to an artist. Inspiration. Maybe it was a coincidence, but since meeting her, he'd come to life again. Once more his work excited him. He had passion and intensity and couldn't wait to pick up a brush each day. Yeah, it sure looked like Shaylee was his little Muse. She had to be, because once she'd appeared on the scene, everything had changed for the better. But that's exactly what made everything such a mess. What about when he left for Europe? If she wasn't there any more, what would happen to his art?

The red light flicked on. Michael poured himself a steaming mug of the black brew and carried it into the open work area.

On the comfy couch by the picture window, he leaned back against the cushions and raked his fingers though his hair. He could ask her to come to Europe with him, but he knew damned well she would refuse unless he first asked her to marry him, which was totally out of the question. He already knew he couldn't give his all to his art while playing the role of a husband. He'd been there, done that, and it hadn't worked. It hadn't been fair to Ashley and it wouldn't be fair to any woman.

But here was Shaylee, slowly crawling right into his heart. Last night when she apologized for rebelling against his instruction, he'd had to fight the urge to take her in his arms. She'd looked so damned sweet. The impudent little pixie. He had to smile. Stubborn and unyielding, just like the daffodils.

After the class, he'd wanted to tell her how he felt about the ignorant comments made by Britney and Helena, but she and Marita left before he had a chance. And now she probably thought he condoned their stupid behavior even though for some time now he'd made a point of discouraging it. But more than likely she hadn't noticed such things. She was always so absorbed in her painting. He almost felt jealous of this concentration that wasn't directed at him.

Good Lord! What was he thinking?

Instead of letting her worm her way into his heart, he should be making an effort to keep away from her. But every time he even thought of that, it totally messed up his gut. Even now the idea made him feel emptier than the mug in his hand.

Michael rose to pour himself some more coffee. Keep away from her? How could he, when every waking hour she was on his mind? He couldn't wait for Monday nights to see her. And as for their "chance encounters" downtown? If she only knew how much rearranging of his schedule he had to do in order for them to "happen". Keep away from her? Not possible.

Last night, after he got home, the phone rang. He'd been too lazy to get up, and instead let the answering machine take it. But when he heard the voice, he jumped up and raced to grab the receiver. Too late. He'd saved the message and played it over and over again, just so he could hear her voice.

"Michael? This is Shaylee. I just wanted to tell you again I'm really, really sorry I was such a jerk tonight. And I hope I run into you on my lunch hour one day this week. Bye."

Yes, she would "run into him" on her lunch hour this week. He would move mountains, if necessary, to arrange it.

Miguel entered the office and sniffed the air. He was a slightly built man, his dark hair brushed smoothly back off his forehead. This, combined with his sensitive, aquiline nose and dark brown eyes, gave him a distinguished, Mediterranean look. Michael had often toyed with the idea of painting Miguel swinging a matador's red cape.

"You're early." Miguel removed his jacket and slipped it on a hanger. "Even the coffee's ready. What gives?" He carried a paper bag into the kitchenette and emptied two fresh muffins onto a plate.

It had become a weekly ritual on Tuesday mornings for Michael to brag about the great things Shaylee had done the evening before. And again, right on cue, he brought up the subject.

"I think Shaylee must be a kind of artistic parallel of Mozart," he began.

"C'mon, Mike," Miguel scoffed. He emerged with a steaming mug in one hand and a blueberry muffin in the other. "Mozart? She can't be that good."

"As a matter of fact, she is. And if she's a neophyte as she claims to be, then she's a rare diamond-in-the-rough. It's a shame I'm leaving for Europe and won't be here to polish her to greatness."

"You're beginning to sound like Henry Higgins," Miguel commented, spreading out the materials for the magazine ad he was working on.

"And what exactly is that supposed to mean?" Michael asked. The words had a strangely familiar ring. Of course! Max and his idiotic Pygmalion idea.

"Well, with all this talk about polishing this 'diamond-in-the-rough' to greatness, make sure you take into account that she may not be thrilled to be your Eliza Doolittle. She may even have a few ideas of her own."

Michael's brow puckered into a frown. "I don't know where everybody gets these weird ideas about Eliza Doolittles and Pygmalions," he retorted.

"Pygmalion? I never mentioned Pygmalion. Who said anything about Pygmalion?"

Michael waved off the idea. "Never mind." He went for a muffin and sat up on the stool at his drafting table. "I'm only trying to teach her as best I can, and if she succeeds in the art world, good for her." He wasn't trying to make her into some great star. Or was he? Still, the idea of mentoring Shaylee and eventually introducing her to Max was damned attractive. Why not?

And if Max was as impressed as Michael expected him to be, well . . . who knew what that could lead to? Eventually a show of her work. But first he'd have to help her to produce something exceptionally fabulous. Teach her to put stronger colour into those delicate paintings of hers. He smiled at her reaction each time he'd suggested such a move.

It would be a challenge for sure, but well worth it.

Chapter Nine

On Wednesday it rained, but Shaylee braved the weather to dash across the street from her office to pick up a sandwich at the deli. Her umbrella kept her clothes dry, but by the time she ran back, her shoes were drenched. She hopped over a puddle, clutching a brown paper bag, but suddenly a pair of strong arms lifted her into the air. She gave a little shriek that changed to laughter when she recognized her kidnapper.

"You should have boots on when you go out in weather like this," Michael admonished her. "Your feet are soaking wet."

Shaylee gave a hasty glance at the amused onlookers. "Please put me down, people are looking."

"I'm parked right here." Without asking, Michael carried her the few steps to his car. He set her down on the sidewalk and opened the door.

Not that Shaylee would have refused to go with him. Ever. Even a few days without him had felt like an empty eternity and she couldn't believe how sweet it was to see him again.

Michael walked around to the driver's side and tossed her umbrella in the back. He got in beside her and closed the door, enclosing them in the intimacy of the car's interior while the persistent rain drummed on the metal. Sitting so close to him, it was almost impossible not to touch him.

"Well now, isn't this a coincidence, meeting you here of all places?" Michael grinned as he pushed the starter and then pulled out into the traffic.

"I didn't think you'd come in weather like this." But she sure had been hoping he would. "I just went across the street to pick up a sandwich." She held up the rain-spattered paper bag. "I'm so annoyed with myself for leaving my lunch on the kitchen counter. The salad's going to be ruined by the time I get home, and I had to spend good money to buy this sandwich." So what if her chatter sounded giddy? She was simply floating with happiness.

"Hey, that happens." Michael reached over to give her hand a squeeze. "No big deal."

Shaylee sighed with contentment. She loved it when he touched her. "It's fine for you to say. You famous artists roll in money."

Michael burst out laughing. "I don't know where you get your facts, but nothing could be farther from the truth. Why do you think I have a day job and teach art on the side?"

Shaylee patted his arm to show her empathy. "Yes, I know art isn't the way to make millions. Maybe you should have been a sports hero or something."

Michael looked rueful. "I'm afraid I've lost my touch for hitting homers. I was hot stuff in the neighbourhood about twenty years ago, but traded my bat for a brush. Now I'm wondering if that was such a smart move."

"Hey, you have wonderful paintings at Max Storm's

gallery." But what about the ones in his atelier? Her attempt at a cheerful smile almost failed and her heart wrenched as she remembered the look on his face that day.

He must have read her mind. "But the stuff in my atelier isn't that great, eh?"

Shaylee's sharp ears picked up a change in his voice. Somehow he didn't sound very despondent.

"Well," she began, but then stopped and sneezed loudly. "Excuse me." She groped for a napkin in the lunch bag.

"That's from running around in the rain, getting your feet wet," Michael scolded her.

She was thankful for the diversion that saved her from replying.

"Actually it's more your style to dunk yourself in freezing rivers up to your neck, isn't it?" he said mischievously.

Shaylee giggled at that, but the memory of what had followed was still as potent as the brandy she'd consumed, and she turned to look out the side window, afraid he would see the haze of love in her eyes.

"You know, you distract me terribly," he said unexpectedly.

Shaylee quickly turned to scan his face, but his eyes were back on the road before she'd had a chance to read their expression. What exactly did he mean by that?

"If I distract you, maybe we shouldn't be meeting like this," she ventured.

"No. You don't understand. When you're not around I keep thinking of you, wondering what you're up to, and I can't concentrate. But when you're near me, I'm okay." He turned to smile at her. "I guess there's only one solution. I'll have to hire you as my model."

"Hah!"

"Paint mixer?"

"I'd mix 'em, all right."

"Wood Nymph?" Michael persisted.

"Sold," Shaylee declared. "Depending on what my duties would be."

"Your duties would be to always be around me so I wouldn't get distracted."

She grinned. "Sounds simple enough."

"How about we celebrate your new job?" And without further ado Michael pulled into the takeout line of the next drive-through donut shop and ordered two coffees and a couple of glazed donuts.

He placed the coffee cups in the cup holders and the donut bag between them. "Let's go down to the lakeshore and watch the storm," he suggested.

They drove the short distance to Lake Ontario, where he parked on a high bluff overlooking the water. As they munched on their donuts, they watched the turbulent waves that crashed against boulders far below them, and burst into foaming spume to be carried off by the driving wind. Heavy raindrops beat against the windshield and were brushed off again and again by the wipers.

Shaylee felt empathy for the waves, breaking against the rocks. Her own heart was in danger of breaking, too. Only three more classes and then she'd never see Michael again. He'd be off to Europe and that would be it.

"You know," he said, "If you really were a Wood Nymph, you'd transform this whole scene and make the sun come out by snapping your fingers."

Smiling, Shaylee did just that, while wishing she

could make her own heart sunny simply by snapping her fingers.

Incredibly, at that moment, a golden glow appeared around the clouds and, while the rain drummed and the wind wailed, the sun made a brief, bright appearance. For one magical moment it bejeweled the lake and transformed each raindrop into a brilliant sapphire. Then, just as quickly, it disappeared and once more the scene turned gray.

Michael stared. "Wow! That was beautiful. How did you do that?"

"I shall never tell," Shaylee stated loftily. "Us Wood Nymphs never divulge our secrets."

Michael covered her hand with his and she could sense tension in his light grip. He opened his mouth to say something, but just then the single hollow gong from a nearby church drifted through the storm.

Shaylee glanced at her watch. "The boss has powers even greater than Wood Nymphs, so I think we'd better start back."

They drove north, away from the lake, and came to a halt in front of Shaylee's office building.

"And make sure you get back to work," Shaylee warned him. She laid her hand on the door handle, but Michael reached over to stop her.

"Listen—" He stopped, took a deep breath and then continued quickly, as though he wanted to get the words out before he changed his mind. "I've got something I want to show you. Do you think I could pick you up after work on Friday?"

Shaylee tilted her head quizzically. "Show me?"

He seemed almost nervous. "Yes, there's something I'd like you to see before—" He stopped and swallowed again.

She knew he was going to say, "before it's all over". An involuntary shiver ran through her.

He gave her a playful tap on the nose. "Hey, don't look so alarmed. I was going to tell you I'll be going to Montréal for a couple of weeks to get the work started on a mural I've designed. But before I go I'd like to show you something. After all, when I get back the classes will be over and—" Again he didn't finish. "So could I?" he asked instead. "Pick you up?"

Shaylee caught her lower lip between her teeth to prevent it from trembling. She wasn't prepared for the flash of pain that shot through her at his words. He was going to Montréal for two weeks, meaning the next lesson would be the last. So the end would come sooner than she'd expected.

"My curiosity is piqued," she managed to say brightly. "Of course you may pick me up."

"Good. I'll be at this very spot five-thirty on Friday."

"I'll be here." She got out and dashed into the building through the rain before he could see her eyes overflow.

On Friday Michael waited anxiously in the foyer of Shaylee's office building, more nervous than a kid about to show his report card to his parents. He'd waited for this moment for two long days. What would she say? What would she think? He hoped confiding in her wasn't a totally bad idea. When he'd trusted her a few weeks back, showing her his lousy art, he'd been afraid it would ruin her regard for him as her teacher. That hadn't happened.

She'd witnessed his near meltdown, so it didn't seem like a huge stretch to trust her again today. If he didn't dare take this chance, he might as well pack up his brushes and cash in his ticket to Europe.

"You look lovely," he said the minute she emerged from the elevator. She wore a sleeveless, light cotton blouse and a short, figure-flattering skirt.

Warmth rose to her cheeks at his words. "Thanks."

At five-thirty the afternoon was still humid and warm, and Michael had ditched his long pants for khaki shorts before he left to pick her up.

Although his stomach was twisted up in a tight knot, he grinned at her as they settled into his car. "I'm happy you agreed to come. I've been thinking about you nonstop."

She turned and surprise flashed in her eyes. Then she smiled. "And I've been thinking about your secret for two whole days. The curiosity has almost killed me."

"I'm hoping you'll like it," he said. "In fact I'm counting on it."

Shaylee clapped a hand to her cheek. "Oh, my. This is getting more mysterious all the time."

She looked around her with interest. "I seem to recognize this area. Are we heading toward your place?"

"Yes. That's where the surprise is." He didn't explain.

"I'm going to miss meeting you on my lunch hours," she said. "Since the classes will be finished by the time you return from Montréal, I guess there won't be any reason for us to meet. That's too bad because I've enjoyed these meetings very much."

She gripped her tote bag handles nervously, and from her chatter he could tell she was apprehensive.

He glanced at her and smiled mischievously. "When I get back from Montréal, I'll have to arrange to bump into you again. Accidentally."

"Arrange? What are you implying? That you arranged these meetings?"

He kept his eyes on the road, but he could hear the disbelief in her voice.

"The way you're talking, one would think you never did have business meetings on those days." She laughed shakily. "The clients were just inventions."

"Well, the first time was for real."

"This is crazy!" Shaylee exploded. But then she bit her lower lip as the situation became clear to her. "But if I really think about it, the meetings have been too numerous to be mere coincidences." Red crept into her cheeks. "Wh-why on earth would you do such a thing?" she stammered.

"Well, what would you've said if I'd phoned you and asked you for a luncheon date?" The car stopped at a red light and Michael turned to look at her. "I know how you feel about me seeing those other women outside the class. You would have thought I was trying to hit on you, wouldn't you?"

She nodded. "Un-huh."

"That's what I thought. So I had to invent excuses."

"But all that trouble, just to have lunch with me?"

"You're worth it."

They reached his house and Michael parked the car in the driveway. As they walked up the front steps, the memories of the last time she was here came flooding back to him and he had to swallow hard. Beside him Shaylee hesitated for a moment before stepping in.

As soon as they were in the hall, he pointed to the stairwell. "The surprise is upstairs," he told her and strode up the stairs eagerly.

Shaylee followed, but he could see she was reluctant to come. She knew where he was taking her, and

she probably didn't want to go through the same unpleasant scenario as the previous time.

They entered the atelier which, Michael knew, must
have looked to her pretty much the same as before.
But he hoped Shaylee would soon notice something
very different.

Damn it all! She wasn't even looking at the paintings. Instead she was concentrating on the mess of un-
washed plates, the paper cups beside the coffee maker,
and probably the same dried donuts still cluttering the
counter.

"I hope those aren't the same cups we drank from
the last time I was here," she quipped. He knew she
was trying to be funny, but he could hear the tremor
in her voice.

"They probably are," he replied. "I've been too busy
to clean up and I don't allow my housekeeper to come
up here and touch anything."

With his stomach in a hundred nervous knots, he
waited. Wasn't she ever going to comment on his
paintings?

Shaylee walked to the counter and absently began
to move a few dirty dishes into the sink. Michael's enthusiasm began to wane as he watched her. Dammit.
What could be so interesting in a couple of crumbling
donuts? She was deliberately not looking at his work.

What did he have to do to get her attention? Tap
dance on the table? When he couldn't stand it any
longer, he had to speak up.

"So, whaddya think?"

She turned to him with a frown. "About . . .?"

Michael swung his arm around the room. "The
paintings, of course." How infuriating could she be?

Now she had to look, and he stopped breathing. His

heart had shifted up to his throat and he tried to swallow it back down.

For a long while she showed no visible reaction as her gaze traveled slowly around the room. It moved from painting to painting, and then started the whole painstaking circuit all over again.

Michael slumped into the armchair and impatiently slung a leg over the arm rest. Why didn't she *say* something? *Anything.* Say they stank. He didn't care.

Was he kidding? Of course he cared. He cared a lot. Her hurtful comments still haunted him, and now he almost wished he hadn't brought her here. God, he didn't want to be hurt like that again. If she said his paintings still lacked soul, she would doom him to a life of murals and ads. He had dared to hope the monkey was finally off his back, but until he heard her say it . . .

At last Shaylee let out a long breath. "Oh, Michael," she sighed. "These are beautiful." She turned to him, her eyes brilliant with joy. "You've done it, haven't you? You've climbed out of the slump."

He sprang out of the chair. "I think so," he said eagerly. "At least I hoped I had. So you really think . . ." He had to swallow hard because the emotion in his throat threatened to choke him. "You think they're as good as the ones you saw at Max's?"

Shaylee came up to him, still beaming, and laid a hand on his arm. It held all the comfort and warmth a man could ever hope to feel in a woman's touch.

"Yes, they're as good," she whispered. "I think they're even better."

He heaved an audible sigh of relief. "Yeah, I think so, too."

He looked at her face, and was touched by the happiness reflected there. If he stroked her flushed cheek, he knew he would be touching pure joy. "After that long dry spell, it sure feels great to have done something I'm honestly proud of."

She smiled. "I'm so happy for you, Michael." Her hand stayed on his arm, radiating a glow right into his heart. "I think you must have discovered your Muse, hiding somewhere in this messy room."

He opened his arms and she slipped into his embrace. Where she belonged. Holding her tightly against him, he whispered against her curls, "Yes, I have. And I want to thank her." He raised her chin so he could look at her face. He hadn't tasted her lips since forever, and now he realized how achingly he'd missed them.

His mouth came down on hers, wanting an answer. Had she missed his kisses, too? And then he knew she had. Her impatient whimper, as her mouth opened for him, told him all he wanted to know.

Shaylee wrapped her arms tightly around his neck and a sweet fire ignited inside her as his kisses deepened. It washed through her, stoked to flames by the heat of his palms, clasping her, fusing their bodies together. She knew how molten rock must feel as it slowly flowed down the side of a volcano. He raised his head to gaze at her. The golden lights in his eyes were dark with passion and the hunger in them matched hers.

"Shaylee." His whisper rasped against her hair. "My Fairy of the Field, you drive me crazy. I can't think of anything but you. Awake or sleeping, it's always your face before me."

The intensity of his words made her gasp. She waited breathlessly for him to tell her he loved her. That he needed her with him. Forever.

"My little Muse," he whispered passionately, and once again his mouth found hers.

But the words she needed to hear remained inside him.

If they even existed.

Shaylee's feet dragged as she climbed up the stairs to the art class. Usually she skipped up, looking forward to seeing Michael again. Yes, she'd finally admitted to herself, *he* was the reason she hurried to class so eagerly each Monday night. But tonight's class would be the last one with him. Sadness weighed on her and she stopped halfway up the stairs, too depressed to continue.

Since last Friday she'd been riding an emotional roller coaster, hoping Michael would call. The kisses they had shared, his whispered words, they *had* to mean something, and she wanted so much to believe they meant he loved her. Her face was always before him, he'd told her, driving him crazy. If that was so, he couldn't possibly leave, never to see her again. Could he?

If he'd told her he loved her, and had asked her to go to Europe with him, like he'd jokingly asked her that day in the park, she would have said yes in a heartbeat. But he hadn't.

Of course he'd made it clear to her he was not into serious relationships, so it was her own fault if she kept this hopeless dream alive. But though she could have kicked herself for her stupidity, she couldn't help it.

For once, Marita reached the green door ahead of her and turned to look back down the stairwell. "What's the matter?"

"I don't know. Somehow I don't feel like painting tonight."

"Oh, come now. Painting always perks you up," Marita said and then added mischievously, "Or at least the teacher does."

But tonight even her friend's joking couldn't lift her spirits and Shaylee was relieved when the evening came to a close. She hadn't accomplished anything. As in the first class, she crumpled up her paper and threw it into the waste basket. Only this time she didn't start anything new, but simply sat there, looking on as Marita struggled with a river.

Michael had stopped by a few times during the evening to look at her work, but his face hadn't revealed even a trace of the passion they'd shared only a few days ago. And here she'd been trying to hide her eyes so he wouldn't see the love shining in them. It stunned her completely that he could be like that. One day he was whispering beautiful words in her ear, and the next he looked at her as though she was nothing more than one of the students.

Shaylee started. God, was that what she was? Was she just another Sue or Britney? Her heart gave a painful squeeze. Had all his whispered words of endearment only been a ruse to lure her into his harem? To "take care of his needs" as he'd expressed it? Was calling her his Muse only been a trick to make her think she was something special to him? Was this all a deliberate game with him? She shuddered. Had she fallen into the very trap she'd been trying to avoid from the beginning?

Shaylee wanted the floor to swallow her, even as Michael asked everyone to listen to his announcement. On the way to class she had been dreading the moment when she'd hear the words that would take him away forever. The words that would signal the end for them. But now, with his strange disregard for her, she didn't know what to think.

"I wanted to let you know," Michael began once the chatter died down, "I won't be here for the last two classes. Sorry about that, but I need to go to Montréal to supervise the start of a mural I designed. I have no choice but to go."

Shaylee turned away so he wouldn't see her face. The moans and groans of disappointment that followed his announcement probably stoked his huge ego. The Lothario. She snorted to herself as she fingered her brushes.

"So are we simply going to muddle through the last two classes without a teacher?" Marita asked. "Or will Shaylee take over?"

Shaylee poked an elbow into Marita's arm. "Shush."

Marita rubbed her arm. "Listen, I know you could do it. But of course, I'm the only one who knows about that pain—"

"*Shush*, Marita."

"What pain is that?" Pauline wanted to know.

"The pain in my arm," Marita quipped and Shaylee giggled at Marita's quick thinking.

Michael raised an eyebrow at this interruption. "Actually, my partner, Miguel Cordova, is coming to teach you. He's been looking forward to seeing how much you all have improved since he was your teacher. And it's time Marita and Shaylee met him. You'll like him."

"Only if he's as good-looking as our present teacher," Marita declared.

Michael chuckled. "Oh, he's much better in every way."

While the others were packing up, Michael approached Shaylee. "Now, you make sure you give Miguel as hard a time as you've given me," he joked. "I want him to see I wasn't exaggerating when I told him what I've gone through every Monday night with you."

Shaylee shook her head. "Nope. I think I'll be as sweet as honey to him. Then he'll wonder what you've been grumbling about."

Michael laughed. "Yes, I believe you would make a liar out of me."

That wouldn't be too hard. As far as she was concerned, he already was one. All his declarations of how she drove him crazy, how he couldn't think of anything but her were nothing but poppycock, as her grandpa would have said.

But then he lowered his head and spoke quietly to her alone. "Would you like to join me at Edwards Gardens on Saturday?"

At his unexpected words she looked up at him with a puzzled frown. What was going on? Wasn't he through trying to trick her?

"I'm not leaving for Montréal until Sunday morning and I wanted to take a look at the spring flowers at the gardens," he explained. "I figure I could snap some pictures now while all the flowers are at their peak. By the time I get back, they may not be as fresh any more."

Although obviously his words were directed only at her, Shaylee glanced quickly around the room. "Are we all going?" she asked.

Marita was busily packing away her materials and, Shaylee suspected, pretended not to have heard the exchange.

"No. Only you and I. If you'll come." He sounded almost shy.

Her breath snagged in her throat. Only a few moments ago she'd been doubting his motives, but now he looked so sincere and the golden lights in his eyes seemed to dance for her alone.

Dimples appeared on his cheeks. "Please?"

Would she be an easily-duped fool if she accepted? Or would she be a distrustful shrew if she refused? Where was the proof he was trying to trick her into becoming one of his groupies? It was only her own suspicious mind making up the scenario because he hadn't shown her any special attention tonight. God, what had she expected him to do? Rush over and take her in his arms and kiss her passionately in front of everyone the minute she walked through the door?

Shaylee gave Michael her sweetest smile. "Yes, I'd like to come."

Was there anything wrong with being in his company once more, even if he hadn't told her what she longed to hear? Maybe he really *did* dream about her. And maybe her face *did* drive him crazy. After all, didn't she dream about him all the time? And wasn't his face driving her crazy as well? And so, since she loved him, maybe he would tell her he loved her, too.

She floated down the stairs while Marita scrambled behind in her stiletto heels.

"Hey, wait up! How come you're in such a hurry *now?* I can't figure you out, you enigma."

Shaylee waited for Marita to catch up. "I'm no enigma. I'm just a simple country girl."

And, at least for now, a very happy one.

After everyone had left, Michael stayed behind to put away the lesson materials. His mind was in complete turmoil. Since Friday, when the evening had ended on such an impetuous note, he'd been treading water, hoping he wouldn't sink under the weight of his feelings.

On the way home, after the passionate kisses he'd shared with Shaylee, they hadn't talked much. But underneath it all he hoped she understood, without him having to spell it out, that this "thing" between them wasn't going to go anywhere. He had no reason to feel guilty. It wasn't like he'd been stringing the little country lass along, because she was quite aware of his "no baggage" rule. They'd talked about it often enough.

Of course he shouldn't have gotten carried away like that in the euphoria of the moment, but those things happened. Especially when she'd been so amazed by his new work. But that didn't change anything. Not his ideas about marriage, nor anything else concerning women. Or her.

In order to give himself time to recover from Friday, and get his head screwed on straight, he'd absolutely refused to allow himself to call her, even though his fingers had itched to select her number. He knew what would follow. They would meet somewhere and things would inevitably heat up between them, like they had in the atelier, and she would probably misunderstand everything. She would think he was going back on his no-commitments policy and would propose to her or something.

Instead he'd gone through a hellish weekend, denying himself the pleasure of her presence.

When he told the class about having to go to Montréal, naturally he didn't add that he hated to leave Shaylee. He'd kept away from her in class tonight, but the thought of not seeing her for fourteen whole days had caused him to slip up and ask her to come to Edwards Gardens.

To look at the spring flowers? As if.

Michael banged the cupboard door shut with enough force to rattle the windows. Damn it all. He wasn't supposed to be feeling this attached to her. He had repeated to himself a hundred times he was *only* interested in her as a student, and he *only* wanted to help her to better herself. But it made no difference. When she was away from him, he missed her so much his gut ached.

And what was more, he couldn't ignore the fact that since she entered his life, his painting had improved incredibly. But was it actually because of *her*, or had he simply got over the dry spell? Yeah, that had to be it . . . Or maybe not . . . How the hell could he know for sure?

What would happen if he went to Europe without her?

Chapter Ten

"Hey, Wood Nymph, great job you've done with the weather," Michael exclaimed as Shaylee climbed into his car and plunked her lunch bag on the back seat.

"Thanks, we aim to please."

For better or worse, it felt so good to be sitting beside him again. Even if this was just an act on his part, at least now her eyes were wide open. If he was sincere, then this could turn out to be a wonderful day. If not, she could still enjoy the outing. Only not quite as much.

Without a shred of doubt, summer had arrived in spirit, if not yet on the calendar. The purring of distant lawnmowers floated in through the open car windows as Michael steered south toward Edwards Gardens. Twenty minutes later he pulled into the parking lot and they stepped out onto the dark pavement that already exhaled pungent warmth. The day promised to be a hot one.

"Let's walk around and see what the groundskeepers have been up to," Michael suggested.

Side by side, they wandered past rosebushes where countless buds promised a blaze of colour in the weeks to come, past beds of tulips of every shade, past newly planted pansies and down to the edge of the lazily-flowing stream, bordered by clusters of forget-me-nots and tall purple irises.

They stopped on a small wooden bridge that arched over the river, and leaned silently against the railing, listening to the cheerful chirps in the trees above. Old weeping willows on the bank reached down to dip their long, leafy tendrils into the water.

Shaylee wanted to touch Michael's arm, so close beside hers. She wanted to feel the coarse hairs on his skin and experience the electrifying thrill that always sparked through her whenever his arm brushed against hers in class.

She picked up a bit of bark and threw it into the river, where it floated away with the stream. It was difficult to imagine today was their last one together. Forever.

Resting her chin on her hands, she took a deep breath. "I can't get enough of all this beauty," she began, in an effort to ease the growing ache inside her. "I look and look, and still there's a hunger in me for more."

"Same goes for me," he murmured, turning to face her. He laid his hand on hers as it rested on the wooden railing. "I look and look, but I can't get enough of you."

Shaylee raised her head, not caring if he saw the love in her eyes. "I was referring to the flowers," she whispered.

"I wasn't." His grip on her hand tightened. "I think you've bewitched me, my little Fairy Princess of the Field."

Her breath caught in her throat at his words but she countered jokingly, "Are you overstepping the teacher-student role again, Mr. Merrick? Like you did a week ago?"

"I thought you were kind of overstepping along with me." He grinned, while the golden lights in his eyes threatened to blind her. "But fine, I won't do it again."

But, oh, how she wanted him to overstep again. Overstep all the way to saying he loved her.

She was ready to say the words, but she first had to hear them from him. If she confessed her love it could lead to a humiliating rejection. And it would put him in an embarrassing position of having to explain to a love-struck woman that he simply wasn't into such commitments. They both remained silent, staring at the slowly flowing river that sparkled in the brilliant sunshine.

But Shaylee didn't want their last time together to be ruined by sadness. She peeked at him impishly. "I could teach you a game that wouldn't overstep any boundaries. Except maybe the child-adult one."

He raised a questioning eyebrow. "Yes?"

"Would you like to play Pooh-sticks?"

"Pooh-sticks? Never heard of it."

"It was invented by a bear who played it with his little piggy friend."

"Sounds freaky." He grinned. "So, what are the rules?"

"They're pretty intricate, but I'll try my best to explain them to you."

She collected a few twigs that had fallen from the weeping willow.

"We stand here by the railing, see?" She enunciated each word very clearly.

He nodded, pursing his mouth in concentration.

"And on a given signal we each drop one stick into

the water. Just one."

"Got it so far. I think."

"Good. You may be brighter than you look. Now here comes the exciting part. As soon as the sticks are dropped, we race to the other side of the bridge, without falling in and—"

"That may be a challenge for you," Michael cut in with a guffaw.

"No smart cracks from the pupils, please. As I said, we run to the other side and . . . ta-da! We see whose stick emerges first from under the bridge."

"And?"

"That's it. But the score keeping is a bit tricky. The best of seven races wins. It's winner take all."

"All what?"

"All . . ." Shaylee pondered. "Whatever the winner decides."

"Fair enough. That should spur me on." A wanton twinkle in his eyes sent a shiver of anticipation through her.

They leaned on the railing, sticks poised.

Michael glanced furtively around him. "I hope nobody's looking. I feel totally ridiculous," he muttered.

"Oh, don't be so worried about your reputation," Shaylee retorted. "This is quite harmless."

"You mean idiotic."

But when Shaylee gave the signal and the sticks were tossed, he was the first on the other side, hanging far over the railing, peering into the shadows beneath the bridge.

"Come on, you slowpoke!" he yelled as he caught sight of his stick. It was swirling in lazy circles, threatening to get caught up in some dry leaves.

Shaylee's stick swam straight and true, emerging

victorious.

She jumped up and down. "I won! I won!"

Michael glowered as his stick finally appeared, very tête-à-tête with a brown maple leaf from last fall. "You traitor," he fumed. "Dallying with a leaf when there's a race to be won."

"You ready for the next round?" Shaylee challenged.

"I certainly am. And this time, look out. This stick is powered by a rocket."

They dropped their twigs, but the rocket failed to ignite and Michael's stick once again came out a sorry second.

"You've probably given me a bunch of faulty sticks," he stormed. "This time I want one of yours and you take this one. It looks like a born loser."

But the born loser turned out to be a winner, and Shaylee clapped her hands, while Michael growled in frustration.

"This race is fixed. You're weaving some of your magic spells, aren't you, you devious Wood Nymph?"

Shaylee smiled sweetly. "No magic spells needed. I'm just an accomplished Pooh-sticker, whereas you're a mere novice. But you're doing quite well for a beginner. And luckily all your sticks have *eventually* come out. If one fails to come out at all, you're skunked."

"That makes me feel better. I think. But I'm going to win the next four if I have to jump in the water and push the damned things out myself."

But that didn't turn out to be necessary, because Michael's twigs easily won the next three rounds.

"This is it," he said as they held their sticks poised for the seventh and final round.

"Go!" Shaylee cried and the two twigs fell into the river with soft splats. She wailed as hers began to swirl toward the bank and was soon hopelessly tangled in the weeds. Michael raced down the embankment and grabbed his winning stick before it could float out of reach.

"I won!" he shouted triumphantly, as he clambered up to the bridge again, brandishing the dripping stick.

Shaylee slapped her forehead dramatically. "I can't believe it. I'm skunked."

Michael put a consoling arm around her. "It's tough being beaten by a rookie, isn't it?"

Shaylee looked up. The ominous fires glowing in his eyes caused flames of anticipation to flare up inside her.

"Now for the prize," he murmured. Slowly he brought his palms up to frame her face. "You did say it's winner take all, didn't you?"

His hands slid to her shoulders and then continued along her bare arms, leaving a trail of burning sparks on her skin. He grasped her wrists and brought her hands behind her in a sign of conquest.

"I won," he whispered.

Shaylee couldn't breathe. She didn't *want* to breathe and break the spell. She wanted to be his captive forever.

Their bodies were only inches apart. Then his face came lower, and finally . . . finally his lips closed the space between them.

The kiss was soft, sensuous. But then a low rumble from his throat signaled his growing passion and he pulled her against him, her hands still in his grip, his lips hard and possessive on hers. As wildfires ignited inside her, she knew she couldn't love him any more if she lived a thousand years.

Just then an animated conversation pierced

through the burning mist that filled her head. Michael released her and his breath came out in a ragged growl. "Damn their timing."

Gasping for air, Shaylee slipped away from his embrace as a small group of tourists came to the bridge, cameras swinging around their necks. They smiled surreptitiously, pretending not to see the lovers.

"Well, that was the best prize I ever got," Michael said with a wry grin after the people had passed. "It's also a thank you for showing me that silly game. Almost as good as the horse races, but not nearly as expensive."

"You're welcome," Shaylee managed to whisper, her limbs still heavy with desire.

"If anyone had told me I'd be here today, at my advanced age, playing a ridiculous game with twigs, I'd have said he's nuts."

"I'm glad you enjoyed it. I'll challenge you to a rematch someday."

But of course that would never be. He was going. She wasn't.

"Yes, we've got to do it again one day," Michael agreed. He held the winning stick up high. "I'm going to keep this forever as a memento of this day," he said. "Oops!"

It fell out of his hand onto the bridge and they both bent down to retrieve it. Michael picked it up and chuckled.

"What's funny?" Shaylee asked, also standing up.

"I was just remembering when we first met with a collision of heads."

"Right!" She rubbed her head. Although she smiled, the memory of their first meeting made her feel oddly melancholic. "How could I forget such an ominous meeting? Hard against hard."

"So you think there was something ominous in that?" Michael asked. His voice was quiet and he no longer smiled.

The sun had retreated behind a cloud, casting a shadow on the river. She watched the water flow along in dark, slow swirls. "Maybe there was," she mused. "We've had our differences, you must admit."

"I don't think it's been all that bad. I mean, we've always managed to clear things up, haven't we?"

He gazed down at her. His lips were so near, and she desperately wanted to feel them on hers again. She swallowed, the taste of desire strong in her mouth. His pupils had darkened, almost hiding the deep blue irises, and she saw her own need reflected in them.

His hand slipped behind her neck and he drew her face close to his.

"I need you, my little Muse," he whispered. "I need you to be with me."

His lips brushed hers and then pressed down, hard. The passionate kiss had the effect of a ton of fireworks going off inside her.

Yet she broke off their kiss and searched his eyes. He needed her? Had she heard correctly?

"You need me?" Her pulse raced with anticipation and she tried to keep her heart from exploding with happiness.

"Yes." Michael held her gaze. "I know I asked you once as a joke, but this time I mean it. Shaylee, you're good for me. Come with me to Europe."

It almost sounded like a proposal. Almost. But the key words were missing. Frowning, she backed out of his arms and he didn't try to stop her.

"Hold on there." Michael held out his palms in a de-

fensive gesture. "Before you shoot me with those dag-
gers in your eyes, just listen for a minute."

"I'm listening," she said gruffly, and took another
step back. She didn't want to hear what he had to say.
Not if his words weren't preceded by, "I love you,
Shaylee."

"We're good for each other. We have so much in
common."

To her the words sounded rehearsed. Good for each
other. So much in common. Great lines.

"You inspire me to paint in a fresh, new way," he
went on. "I haven't figured out how it's happened, but
I only know after you came into my life, I haven't had
any desire to . . . to consort with any other women."

"With any *other* women?" She glowered at him. "As
in now you're only consorting with me? Like on Friday?
And like just now?"

But he pressed on, ignoring her scornful words.
"That's not how I meant it. Just listen, please. Since
the first time you were in my atelier, I haven't had the
desire to do anything but paint."

He smiled, and Shaylee's knees almost buckled beneath her. If he thought he could use his dimples to
win her over, it wasn't going to work. She turned away.
Those golden lights in his eyes weren't going to work,
either.

He continued to entreat her, more softly now.
"Shaylee, please come to Europe with me. I need you.
You're good for me."

Disappointment mixed with anger flared through
her. He had his nerve! "You need me?" Shaylee's voice
seethed with contempt. "Well, Michael, this isn't just
about you and *your* needs. It's not just about me helping you with my so-called inspirational powers. It may

surprise you to learn that I have my own agenda in life, with my *own* goals and aspirations, and my *own* needs. And they don't include *you*." Liar. She wanted her plans to include him. She wanted that more than anything.

He stared at her, genuine surprise on his face, obviously taken aback by her venomous reaction. Obviously the man honestly hadn't expected her to refuse his offer. Could he be any more self-centered?

"All you are concerned with is how I can serve your needs. And how could I do that, pray tell? As your model? Your paint-mixer? Or hey, maybe I could . . . nudge-nudge, wink-wink . . . take care of those *other* needs? Hmm?"

She knew she was being crude, but at this point she didn't much care. "You're pretty selfish and brazen to even ask me. So now, if you'll excuse me, I have things to do and places to go, *without* you."

She turned to walk away, but before she'd gone more than a few steps, Michael grabbed her by the arm and swung her around to face him.

"Shaylee, stop that! This isn't just about me. We would *both* benefit from going to Europe. I understand you have your dreams and I can help you achieve them. I have connections and influence, and I can give you a boost up the ladder. Don't you see?"

Yes, she could see. But she could also see when they returned from Europe, she'd be left like a piece of forgotten luggage on the carousel.

Yet when Michael drew her into his arms, she allowed it to happen. She didn't have the strength nor the willpower to resist. But although she wanted to melt against him, she managed to hold her ground. No way would she bend to his terms. She stood there, stiff and motionless.

"We'd be together in Europe for a whole year," Michael whispered softly against her hair.

"A whole year, you say!"

He either didn't hear, or he ignored the sarcasm in her voice. He raised her chin and looked earnestly into her eyes. "Yes, we could do a lot of damage in the art world in a year. I could be your mentor and take you with me to all the places where artsy people hang out. You have extraordinary talent and I can help you become something great. I know it."

Shaylee froze.

There! Finally the words she'd been dying to hear from him were out. Extraordinary talent. The thought almost made her dizzy. With him as her mentor, helping her learn the ropes, connect with the right people . . .

Or was he only saying that so he could get her to come with him? That had to be it. Why else would he only now, finally, tell her how great she was, instead of saying so in class? Smart move, but she wasn't going to fall for it.

Even if he really meant it, she wasn't ready to pay the price for being with him for a year, intimately together by day and making love at night. Because of course that's what it would come to. From the way their bodies reacted when they kissed, sex would be unavoidable. They'd come very close to it that day in his atelier, and she knew she wouldn't be strong enough to resist him. And he certainly wouldn't put up any roadblocks to sex. Then, when they returned to Canada he would simply drop her.

She struggled, but his arms held her in a tight grip.

"I'm not going with you."

But he obviously had no intention of freeing her. "Shaylee, listen—"

"Let me go," she said sternly, and this time he obeyed. "Michael, I'm not a naïve, innocent Wood Nymph. I know our relationship in Europe wouldn't be platonic. You know I want you. You've felt it and I'm not going to deny it. The problem is, when we return to Canada you'd drop off your baggage—which would include me—and traipse off to live your life again as artist Michael Merrick, carefree bachelor with no permanent ties."

His face went dark. "I've told you how I feel about that. I said it at the very beginning so there wouldn't be any misunderstanding."

"That's right, you did. But where do you draw the line? A year together would be all right, but after two years would it start to feel too permanent? What about five years? How exactly does it work with you?"

Michael didn't reply and Shaylee went on, though her voice quivered, threatening to break. "I can't play these games with you, Michael, because . . . because I love you too much."

There, she'd said it. Shaylee tore out of his arms, turned and ran. She could almost hear her heart breaking.

Because he didn't try to stop her.

Luckily a bus came along just as she reached the park gates. She dashed the short distance to the bus stop, got on, paid her fare, and sank into a seat far from the other passengers. Under the guise of blowing her nose, she furtively wiped away her tears.

Her heart twisted with pain. He hadn't returned her words of love. He had simply let her go. She wiped her eyes again. And again.

Obviously Michael only cared for her as someone who could be useful to him. His heart wasn't involved at all. After all he'd said, her hopes had soared that today he finally would say—. A bitter laugh escaped her, sounding more like a sob. She blew her nose again.

This was it, then.

Shaylee hid her amusement as Britney began to cast beguiling glances in Miguel's direction the moment the man entered the studio. He was ready prey for the women Michael had lately been neglecting.

"Hello, Miguel," Britney crooned. "It's so wonderful to see you again." Her lush lips formed into a pout. "You haven't been around here enough. You could have dropped in to visit a few times, you know."

Marita drew in a breath. "Wow! Have you ever seen a more gorgeous pair of brown eyes?" she whispered. "No man has a right to have such long, dark lashes. A woman with lashes like that wouldn't even need to use mascara. Am I drooling yet?"

Shaylee grinned and patted Marita's shoulder. "Down, girl, down."

"Oh, just let me feast my eyes on that slim matador. Men like that don't come along every day."

The way Miguel firmly but politely deflected Britney's overtures, made Shaylee immediately warm up to him. He greeted each of his old students individually before finally coming to the table where Shaylee and Marita were setting up.

"So, you're the young lady Michael's been raving about for weeks," Miguel said with a heart-stopping smile. "He's told me a lot about his great find."

Great find? "What do you mean?" Shaylee asked,

trying to sound casual and not let her surprise show.

Miguel laughed. "I swear he thinks he's Henry Higgins and has found his Eliza Doolittle. The way he tells it, it sounds like *he's* been the one doing all the hard work, trying to make you into something great so he can then show you off as his masterpiece."

Although this was all said lightly, with a chuckle, Shaylee was stunned by the words.

Where had she heard this before? In Edwards Gardens, of course, when Michael said he could be her mentor and help her become something great. Fury almost made her choke.

"Michael said that?" she stammered when she finally got her vocal chords to co-operate. How dare Michael say such things to Miguel but never to her?

Marita coughed nervously, clearly prepared to stop the conversation if it became too inflamed.

"Oh, maybe not in so many words," Miguel amended with a wave of his exquisitely fine hand. "But the way he carries on, I get the impression he would love to take you places and show you off. You know, like Henry Higgins did."

"Oh that's rich," Britney broke in with a sarcastic laugh. "Michael's been watching too many reruns of 'My Fair Lady'."

To Shaylee, Miguel's words were like a kick in the stomach. Not only did Michael want her along with him in Europe for his own selfish needs—as his Muse and his sex companion—but he also wanted to show her off as his Eliza Doolittle at those artsy places he'd talked about. It wasn't about helping her, as he'd claimed, but about brandishing her as a feather in his own cap.

Could the man really be so selfish and callous? So

uncaring of another's feelings? Shaylee didn't want to believe it, but that's what Miguel's words implied.

Her fists curled in anger. So Michael wanted to make her into his masterpiece, did he? Her mouth pursed into a tight line. Well, she would show him a masterpiece—her painting on the wall! Her very own work, done before she'd even heard of Michael Merrick. She would show him she wasn't anyone's Eliza Doolittle, and she didn't need any Henry Higgins to recreate her into anything.

She drew in a deep, angry breath, but before the explosion could happen, Marita intervened. "And tell me, what has Michael said about my work?"

Her words diffused the situation and Shaylee exhaled her fury.

Grinning, Miguel turned his attention to Marita. "Ah, yes, he's told me about you, too."

Marita's reply came laced with her usual deadpan humour. "His brightest star, right?"

Miguel laughed. "Yes, he's told me *exactly* how good you are."

"See? I knew it!" Marita exclaimed proudly, poking Shaylee with her elbow.

Miguel laughed and patted Marita on the shoulder. "Michael thinks the world of you, and I can see why."

The class under Miguel was different. He didn't start with a demonstration lesson, but urged everyone to continue with whatever they'd been doing the week before. Shaylee pulled out a painting she'd been working on at home.

Miguel came up behind her. "That's beautiful, Shaylee. I love the way you've captured the sun as it appears from behind the clouds."

Pleasure flooded through Shaylee at these words.

Miguel thought it was beautiful? Michael's praise had never contained such adjectives. She squeezed her eyelids tightly shut, but tears forced their way out. Sure, in the park he'd told her she had extraordinary talent, but he had only said it to lure her into coming with him to Europe.

Miguel's enthusiasm was almost intoxicating, and Shaylee eagerly ate up every word. Soon she was totally absorbed in her work, only vaguely aware of Miguel coming to stand silently behind her from time to time.

She painted with a glow inside her as the picture took shape under her brush. A calm harbor, surrounded by a deep green forest. The setting sun mirrored on the dark waters of the bay. A sailboat moored for the night, the sunlight reflecting from the water playing on its blue hull. Another boat entering the bay, sails aglow in the sunset, looking for an anchorage.

"This is a masterpiece, Shaylee," Miguel said, as once more he stood behind her.

Everyone gathered around to see what so impressed their teacher.

"Have you done other paintings like this one?" Miguel asked.

Before Shaylee had a chance to stop her, Marita blurted out, "You should see the great painting she's got on the wall in her living room."

"Is that right, Shaylee?" Miguel asked.

"Well, there is a painting," Shaylee replied, her cheeks heating up. "But I don't know how *great* it is." The euphoric feeling was beginning to desert her, replaced by fear. Was this it? The moment she would finally expose herself to the world. Or at least to a professional artist.

"Do you think you could bring it next week?" Miguel placed an encouraging hand on her shoulder, as though sensing her apprehension.

Her fear and doubt evaporated and Shaylee's heart sang with excitement. Yes, she could! And she *would*. Hadn't she come to Toronto for this very reason? Would she allow herself to self-destruct at the very moment when fate was ready to give her a push in the direction she'd been striving to go all her life? Would she blow this wonderful chance?

No way!

Her answer held a wallop of defiance. "Yes, I'll bring it."

Chapter Eleven

The following Monday night Shaylee lugged a large parcel, wrapped in brown paper, up the stairwell. At the landing she stopped in front of the murky green door, now missing a few more paint chips. She felt almost as nervous as she had when she'd come for her first lesson.

All the way to the studio on the bus she'd prayed that Miguel would be kind and not say anything disparaging about her beloved painting. It was one thing to act out of defiance, but another to finally expose her dearest secret to the critical eyes of an expert.

Marita held the door open for her when they entered, and Shaylee sighed with relief to find Miguel hadn't arrived yet. She almost hoped he wouldn't be coming at all and the painting could remain in its wrappings. She placed it near the coat rack by the door, on the off-chance Miguel might forget he'd asked her to bring it.

But as soon as he arrived and had apologized for being late, he immediately looked around for the painting. "Did you bring it?" he asked eagerly.

Shaylee hesitated, just long enough for Marita to blurt out, "Yes, she did. Shaylee, why don't you place it here on the table and lean it against the wall so everyone can see it. Personally I think it's absolutely fabulous."

Embarrassed, Shaylee gave a short dry laugh. "Marita thinks she's a professional art critic."

"Well, let's see if she's right," Miguel said.

Shaylee carefully removed the paper from around the painting and carried it to the table. This was it. No one but Marita and her family had ever seen this work but now the whole world would get a chance to critique it. Well, maybe not the whole world, but at least one discerning person. And the class. Drawing a deep breath to fortify herself, Shaylee turned the painting around and propped it up against the wall.

Total silence followed. For a long time no one spoke and Shaylee felt herself slowly sink through the floor. They were too kind to say anything. She was about to pick up the painting and take it back to the corner, when Miguel gave a soft whistle.

"Marita, I believe you're right," he breathed.

Shaylee's heart leapt back to life. "She is?"

Beside her, Marita glowed with satisfaction. "What did I tell you?"

"You did this?" Miguel asked. His face registered total amazement.

"Yes." Shaylee pointed at the signature.

"Shaylee," he read. "Just Shaylee."

"That's how I always sign my paintings. I don't think there are too many Shaylees around. And I doubt many of them paint in watercolours."

"Yes, yes, of course," Miguel muttered, rubbing his chin as he continued to inspect the details of the painting. "It's amazing. It lives. The breath of the evening breeze is there, in the trees, on the leaves." He straightened up. "It's a wonder Michael hasn't raved more about your work. He's seen this, I assume?"

Shaylee hesitated. "No, he hasn't."

"Well, you should've shown it to him." Miguel walked away from the painting and looked at it from afar, nodding his handsome, dark head.

She couldn't tell Miguel that because of Michael's critical comments, she hadn't felt confident enough to show him her beloved painting. Perhaps she'd been too thin-skinned and had taken his criticism too much to heart, but she'd so desperately wanted to hear just one "Wow!" from him. That would have been enough to give her courage to show him this painting, as well as the others she had stored under her bed.

But his "Wow!" had come too late. And for the wrong reason.

"Oh, Shaylee, that's fab," Sue almost screeched. "I don't know how you did it."

Helena gave Shaylee a hug. "That's superior, dear."

Britney scrutinized the signature. "It's very good," she finally conceded. "*If* you did it yourself."

"And if I didn't?" Shaylee couldnt help the quip.

"It's still very good," Britney threw over her shoulder.

Burt and Bruce each said, "Hmmm." And then. "Uh-huh. Brilliant."

Even Peggy came to take a look, nodded, and then went off to work on her own masterpiece.

For the rest of the evening the painting stood on the table and Tracy and Pauline never seemed to get tired of returning to gush over it. Shaylee felt she'd died and gone to heaven.

At last it had happened. A professional artist had admired her work.

The wheels of the storage container squealed as Shaylee dragged it out from under her bed. Slowly she removed the protective plastic covering and then, sitting on her knees, she carefully picked up one of the watercolours and propped it up against the bed. A field dotted with beautiful flowers, a rock and a fallen tree trunk in the foreground. But in the distance, dark clouds were gathering, threatening to obscure the sun. A storm was approaching.

She nodded and breathed a satisfied sigh. Tenderly she picked up another painting and placed it beside the first. Then one by one she took all the paintings out of the storage container and stood them up. Each picture told of the peace and beauty of the farm country she loved. By the time she'd inspected the last of the dozen works, her legs had gone to sleep under her. Stiffly she rose onto her numb feet and hobbled to the kitchen.

She took a glass out of the cupboard and poured herself a drink of water. This was it. What had happened in class tonight could change everything. She couldn't help wondering what might have ensued if she'd obeyed Marita and brought the painting to class weeks ago. What would Michael have said? What would he have done?

Shaylee shrugged. Michael's opinion no longer mattered. He was out of the picture and soon he'd be leaving for Europe. But though she was angry with him, a wistful sadness filled her. If only things could have been different. And foolishly, despite his rejection of her in the park, she couldn't help dreaming he would call from Montréal and tell her he had changed his mind.

But he hadn't. And she called herself a silly fool.

She straightened her shoulders and took a deep breath. Tomorrow morning, before she lost her nerve and before the euphoria of tonight had worn off, she would take a couple of her paintings to Max Storm.

What would Max think of them? What would he say?

Well, whatever the outcome, she knew her life was about to change forever. Either she would release the Genie out of the lamp, and it would give her what she'd always coveted, or she would open Pandora's box, and her world would come crashing down around her.

Shaylee wandered back into the bedroom and looked at the paintings scattered around her. She sighed deeply. Somehow her goal had changed from when she first came to Toronto. No longer would being a professional artist totally fulfill her dreams. She had become greedy. Now she wanted recognition and Michael. Too bad that part of her dream would always remain unfulfilled.

Why couldn't the Genie do its number on him? Shaylee fully understood Michael's need to immerse himself in his art, because she had the same need. But why couldn't Michael see that if he loved her, they could be a very compatible couple? Hadn't he even said they had a lot in common? The problem, of course, was with the word *if*. Since he didn't love her, it was a moot point.

Deep in thought, Shaylee began to put the paintings back in the box. With or without Michael, she was about to take the most important step of her life. She'd heard the words she'd been waiting to hear, although they'd come from Miguel instead of Michael, and now the next step was hers to take alone.

Tomorrow she would bring her work to Max Storm.

Michael lay in the king-size bed in his hotel room and looked at the red figures of the alarm clock on the night table. Six-thirty.

He yawned. He hadn't slept well, which had pretty well been the state of things ever since Shaylee had left him standing in the park. His brain buzzed with thoughts of her and what had happened. And what she'd said.

I love you too much.

During the two weeks in Montréal he hadn't been able to get those words out of his head. Throughout the day, even while conferring with his client, or talking with the people who would be working on the mural project, his mind had been at Edwards Gardens. And each night in his hotel room he'd been going over every detail of that conversation. And what his response should have been. And what an idiot he was.

She loved him. He'd never expected to hear that, and it opened up a whole new scenario for him. He'd told her he only wanted her to come to Europe as his Muse, but if he'd had the brains and the courage to look deep into his own heart weeks ago, he would have realized this wasn't true at all. Plain and simple, he wanted her to come because he'd fallen in love with her. No way could he deny that fact any longer.

But that's not what he'd told her, was it? He'd allowed her to believe he would cavalierly drop her out of his life after they returned home. What did he really mean by his long-held conviction about no permanent relationships? Shaylee had hit the nail on the head when she'd asked him where, exactly, he drew the line. At what point would he feel the relationship was becoming too permanent and start to feel like he was married again? Two years down the road? Five?

The idea of her coming to Europe with him for a year and then simply ending it all on their return, now sounded totally selfish, even cruel. No wonder she'd balked at his suggestion. She should have been repulsed by it. It certainly repulsed him. How could he have treated her like this? Because of her, he had been happy and fulfilled, and once again painted with passion and emotion. He felt excited, like in his younger days, before his marriage had made him cynical and soured his outlook on relationships and love.

Michael sat up in bed. What a fool he'd been. Shaylee had showed him the way back to his creative self and he'd tossed her aside, rejecting her love. He had to call her right now, before she left for work, and say to her what he should have said in Edwards Gardens.

"I love you, Shaylee!"

Michael shouted the words aloud. It was true. No other explanation existed for the way he felt whenever she was around, or for the way he missed her when she wasn't. The thought of sailing to Europe and leaving her behind seemed like the most idiotic thing he could ever do.

How could he think of leaving her? Being without her even for these two weeks had seemed like an eternity. Never mind a whole year. She would probably meet some guy and be totally involved with him— maybe even married—by the time he returned from Europe. Just thinking about that made his stomach clench with an urgent fear. If only he wasn't too late. If only she would accept his apology.

His phone rang. He groped for it on the bedside

table but his hand came up empty. Where was the damned thing, anyway? And who the hell was trying to reach him at this hour?

"Shut up already," he mumbled, stumbling out of bed. He followed the annoying sound into the closet, where his jacket hung from last night's dinner with his client. The breast pocket was ringing.

"Yeah? Hello." This had better be good.

"Michael!" Miguel exclaimed. Even from the single word, Michael could tell his partner was very agitated.

His concern rose. "What's wrong?"

"It's Shaylee."

Shaylee! In a blinding flash the last dregs of sleep vanished from his brain. His body was ready to spring to action, but his legs were threatening to turn to jelly. His mouth felt like he'd swallowed sand.

"What happened to her?" he managed to croak.

"Why didn't you tell me?" Now Miguel's voice was more excited than agitated.

Michael shook his head in an effort to understand. "What the hell are you talking about? Why didn't I tell you what?" At least it didn't sound like Shaylee was in the hospital—or worse.

"That she's such a great artist."

"You phoned me at six-thirty in the morning to tell me that?" Anger replaced the fear that had nearly made him throw up. "Couldn't you contain your excitement till I got back tomorrow night? Besides, I've told you she's talented. Every week after class I've repeated ad nauseam the woman is damned good."

"Yes, you told me she's good, but you never told me she's *great*."

Michael ran his fingers through his tousled mop. "Good-great. Great-good. What's the difference? Yes, I think she has exceptional potential. So what's your point?"

Ignoring Michael's irritated voice, Miguel went on. "The fresh and unique way she portrays ordinary landscapes. I tell you, it's incredible. You never did see that painting she had on her wall in her apartment, did you?"

Michael rubbed the final shreds of sleep from his eyes. What in damnation was going on? What painting was Miguel blathering on about? Michael didn't want to show his ignorance, so he said nothing and waited for Miguel to clarify the issue.

"She brought it to class," Miguel continued. "I tell you, the woman is brilliant. She blew me over."

Michael held the phone away from his ear, so he, too, wouldn't be blown over by Miguel's excitement. And then Miguel said something that made Michael's eyes fly wide open.

"I guess she called you about going to see Max?"

The silence at Michael's end obviously told the story.

"No? I thought she would've," Miguel went on. "Well, it seems she marched right up to The Four Winds Gallery with a couple of paintings under her arm. Max called me last night and told me how impressed he was."

The dead silence at Michael's end continued. The news had literally struck him dumb.

Miguel waited for a while and then, more hesitantly, he said, "Sorry. I'm sure she was going to call you. I didn't mean to beat her to the punch. I naturally assumed she would have called you right away, you being her teacher and all. She'll probably call you today and here I've spoiled her surprise. I hope she won't be annoyed with me."

Michael imagined his partner squirming with excitement, while he sat, staring at his cell phone like it had turned into a strange, new specimen right there in his hand. Nothing made any sense. But he wasn't about to let Miguel know he was sitting here, feeling like he'd walked into a theatre with the production in full swing. He had to play for time until he caught on to what exactly was going on.

"You called me at six-thirty in the morning to tell me that?" he scoffed, pretending indifference.

But Miguel's excitement couldn't be suppressed. "It seems Max immediately said he wants to include her in his upcoming show."

Michael didn't want to hear any more. Anger made his empty stomach growl. Shaylee had shown some incredible work to Miguel and to Max.

But not to him, her teacher!

Miguel went on. "I'm not surprised Max was impressed. If the rest of her work is as good as the painting she brought to class, she's a real gem."

Stymied, Michael listened. His day had barely begun, but already night was returning, with his thoughts getting darker by the minute. What the hell was this all about? How come she'd never told *him* about these super-fabulous paintings?

"I was going to take her to Max when I felt she was good and ready," Michael finally said defensively. "You had no business taking her."

Miguel laughed. "*I* didn't take her to Max. She made that decision all on her own. She's a beautiful, gutsy little lady. Listen, Henry Higgins, I'm afraid your Eliza has flown the coop."

"Will you stop with that Henry Higgins stuff!"

Michael's voice rose in anger. "And you do realize, don't you, that you overstepped your role as a temp? I'm her teacher. You encroached on *my* territory."

"Your *territory*?" Miguel retorted. "Since when do you consider your students your territory? Does she somehow belong to you?"

Michael swallowed and his anger deflated like a pricked balloon. He remained silent. Miguel was right. Shaylee didn't belong to him.

"*I* asked her to bring that painting to class so I could see it. *You* didn't," Miguel went on. "I saw right away how great it was. And I told her so."

"You had no right—" Michael began but knew he sounded absolutely stupid. "I'm her teacher," he muttered, utterly defeated.

"Listen, what could I do? Here I was shown a painting that simply blew me over."

"Yeah, yeah, you already said that. And now, if you'll excuse me, I'll get back to sleep."

"You know, she's not only talented, she's also very beautiful," Miguel continued, as though the sole purpose of this call was to torment Michael. "And I'm going to ask her—"

"Keep your hands off her," Michael growled darkly.

"Why? I don't remember you telling me you're interested in her other than as a student. Or have I missed something?"

If Miguel had been in the room, Michael would've had him flat on the floor by now. "Listen, you Spanish Casanova!" he shouted. "Don't you even dare to think—"

"Unless you're in love with her yourself?" Miguel cut in with irritating calmness.

Yes, I am! Michael wanted to shout, but instead he

ground out, "Go to hell, Cordova," and snapped the phone shut.

The mattress heaved as he fell back onto the bed.

Shaylee had revealed some fabulous painting. To Miguel. Not to him. Michael got up again and walked around the confines of the hotel room in his boxers, his fists clenching and releasing in agitation. He felt like an outsider. Like the kid who hadn't been invited to the birthday party.

And to top it off, it sounded like Miguel was interested in dating Shaylee. Well, he could have her. The woman was full of lies. Putting on a good show about being a neophyte, an unschooled painter, and then turning out to be a pro. At least according to Miguel. And now Max.

Thank God he hadn't called her this morning. It would have been a pretty embarrassing situation with him gushing to her about his love, and all the while she'd been playing games with him. Showing Miguel and Max a fabulous painting of hers behind his back. *Supposedly* fabulous, anyway.

He slumped heavily onto the bed and grasped his head with his hands. How could she have done this? Why hadn't she told *him* of the work she had at home?

Because she didn't trust him. The realization struck him like a powerful fist straight to the solar plexus. *He* had taken a huge leap of faith with her and brought her up to his atelier to see his lousy work. *He* had blindly trusted she wouldn't stomp on his self-esteem, and would be perceptive enough to realize how showing her these paintings took a helluva lot of courage on his part. And now it was obvious she hadn't trusted him enough to show him her work.

But what hurt most was she'd shown it to *Miguel*, a

man she'd barely met. And not to Michael, her teacher. Her friend. Or so he'd thought.

Damned Miguel!

Michael punched the mattress and wished it were his *former* friend's face. He sprang up from the bed and paced the room like a caged tiger. Agitated, he bumped his foot on a bedpost. Dammit! Jumping on one foot, he grabbed his throbbing big toe and massaged it.

He wanted to hate Shaylee for leading him on, and making him believe she was all honesty and sincerity. For letting him think she was listening to his lessons so attentively, while all the while she already was an accomplished artist. Mendacity, that's all it was. Duplicity. Lies. She never needed him. Or his lessons.

He collapsed heavily into the armchair and ran a hand across his face. He wasn't about to blubber about this. It wasn't worth it. What a hellish situation it was. He needed to get his priorities straight right now and not allow a pair of huge violet eyes make him forget what was the most important thing in his life. His art.

He *didn't* need her. The dry spell was over, and getting his mojo back had nothing to do with her. All that rot he'd been spouting about her being his Muse. Michael snorted. He would set her straight as soon as he got back to Toronto.

He rose to face the day, but it looked more like night had fallen again.

Shaylee unscrewed a small tube of Brown Madder, but suddenly she stopped and swallowed a sob. Her eyes threatened to fill.

"Michael laughed so hard when I told him about

Brown Madder," she told Marita.

On the other side of Shaylee's kitchen table, Marita put a few finishing strokes on her sketch. "When was that?"

"The first time we chatted as friends, on that snowy evening in March. Remember I *told* you about it? I threw a snowball at a telephone pole and hit it smack on." She didn't tell Marita how the golden lights in his eyes had danced under the glow of the street lamp, but she remembered every detail.

And here she was, totally miserable. Disappointed and angry, too. She'd told him she loved him and he hadn't said anything. He'd let her walk out of his life without so much as a friendly wave.

The sadness gnawing at her heart even threatened to dim the euphoria of the past few days. This was so unfair. She'd worked hard for this moment and dreamed about it for years, and now that it had arrived she wasn't as happy as she had every right to be. She should have been floating on a rainbow-coloured cloud, shouting from the rooftops for all of Toronto to hear, and all the way to Kitchener, "I have arrived! I am good. Max loves my work!"

But Michael wasn't here to share her joy and that seemed to take the glow out of everything. She wished it weren't so, but her brain couldn't make her silly heart see things in a more cheerful light.

Shaylee looked out the window and sighed. No wonder she was so depressed. Even the weather did its best to make her sad. A frustrated wind whipped rain against the windows, and its angry gusts now and then gave the panes a rattling shake. Through the rain-beaded windowpanes the city looked tearful and out of focus. That didn't help one bit.

She had taken the paintings to Max four days ago. He'd fallen in love with them at first sight, and now planned to include them as part of a show featuring two other young artists. "Troika of Rising Stars" he now called the show. It had originally been called "Duo of Rising Stars" but after seeing Shaylee's work, Max was adamant he would also include her.

"I believe you'll be the star of the show," he'd enthused to Shaylee's delight and amazement. She? The star of the show? She'd be happy just to have her work hanging anywhere in the gallery. Even in the basement.

Because of the show, she'd been totally engaged the last few days, which was a blessing, because otherwise she would have been moping in misery. The knowledge that Michael had wanted to use her for his own ends— that selfish Henry Higgins—hadn't succeeded in extinguishing her love. And though she'd called herself a gullible imbecile, and every other suitable name under the sun, none of it had helped. She still loved him.

Shaylee exhaled in resignation. She might as well get used to this emptiness in her heart, because it was there to stay.

For two days now Michael had been back from Montréal, and Shaylee had half-expected him to call. Her silly heart was hoping against hope that while he was away from her, he would realize he did love her after all. But he hadn't called.

"Well, as far as I'm concerned, he can continue his love affair with his art and go to Europe on his own," she snapped. "I've achieved what I set out to do when I first came to Toronto. And no thanks to him."

Marita looked up from her work and her mouth curved slightly. "I agree with you, but I think you can thank him for *something*." She grinned as Shaylee vigorously shook her head. "Yes, you do, because that Henry Higgins business made you so angry and defiant you finally got up the nerve to show Miguel your painting."

"I guess that's true." Shaylee chose a brush and wet it. "And then I was *going* to tell Michael that *Miguel* thought my painting was excellent, so whaddya say *now*, Mr. Teacher? You still want me to apply a touch of Sepia?"

Yes, that's exactly what she would have said to him, *if* Michael had called after returning from Montréal. But he hadn't.

"Are you really planning to wet your whole paper with that little brush? That'll take you all evening," Marita pointed out.

Shaylee looked at the long, narrow rigger in her hand and burst out laughing. "Shows I'm not all here, doesn't it?" She stuck the rigger back in the jar and chose a wide hake brush instead.

"Well, you do have a good reason for being distracted," Marita said. "With the show. And all."

Shaylee knew Marita's "and all" referred to Michael, but for once her friend was discreet enough not to mention him.

Straightening her back, she wet the paper with extra care and squeezed out a blob of the Brown Madder that had set her reminiscing. Time to concentrate on her work and stop this daydreaming. And the night-dreaming, too. She rested her cheek on her hand. Well, her goal was within sight at long last, even if Michael wasn't around to see.

She still hadn't dabbed her brush in the pigment, and noticed her paper was getting dry.

Marita held up her work. "What do you think of this? Is there anything *majorly* wrong with it? Never mind the details."

"No, it looks all right. I think you've made quite a bit of progress in the last ten weeks. How does my sketch look?"

"Terrible, as usual."

Shaylee grinned. "Thanks." It was nice to have Marita here to keep her company, so she wouldn't think about Michael all the time.

"Can you imagine!" she exclaimed, determined Michael was now off the agenda for the night. "My paintings are actually going to be part of a real art show. And at a real gallery, too. I still can't believe Max liked my paintings so much."

"And here you were questioning my credentials as an art critic," Marita crowed.

Shaylee bowed her head. "I humbly apologize for doubting your expertise."

Just then there was a loud knock on the door.

Shaylee looked at Marita with a frown. She didn't usually have unexpected visitors at this late hour.

"Could be one of my brothers," she mused. "Though none of them called to say they were in the city."

She crossed to the door and squinted through the peephole. Waves of pleasure flooded through her. Michael! She'd given up hope of ever seeing him again, and here he was. Was it possible that in the two weeks he'd been away, he'd had a change of heart?

But then, even through the tiny opening, she was able to study his stance. His mouth was in a tight line and she guessed there would be no golden lights dancing in his eyes. Her stomach clenched in fearful anticipation. He did not look like an eager lover.

She whirled around to face Marita.

"What is it?" her friend asked in alarm. "Who is it?"

Shaylee's voice failed her completely. "It's . . ." Her lips suddenly felt parched. "Michael," she croaked. She didn't make a move to open the door.

"So, let the man in," Marita said and began to gather up her painting materials.

Shaylee realized Marita was planning to leave her alone to face Michael. "Please, Marita, stay," she appealed and spread her hands out before her.

Marita shook her head emphatically. "Uh-uh." She quickly filled her bag and headed toward the door. And as Shaylee still hadn't opened it, Marita did it for her.

"Hello, Michael," Marita said cheerfully. Michael stood there, hands deep in the pockets of his jeans. "I didn't realize you were coming. But I was on my way out anyway. Bye."

Without waiting for his reply, she headed down the hall toward the stairwell, leaving Shaylee to stand there on legs that threatened to turn into jelly under her.

Michael looked after Marita and then, slowly and deliberately, turned back to Shaylee. He leaned his tall body against the door frame and folded his arms across his broad chest.

"So, how've you been?" His voice was casual, but the steely glint in his eyes told her something hard lurked beneath the words.

Shaylee's mouth felt coarse as sandpaper. The biceps at her eye-level looked powerful and she remembered how wonderful his arms had felt holding her. She prayed her voice wouldn't fail. "Fine. How're you?" she finally managed to say in a reasonably normal tone.

His slow movements reminded her of an animal on the prowl and she half-expected him to bare his teeth. A thrill, like she'd once experienced on a wild carnival ride, tingled down her spine. It contained an element of both excitement and danger, making her limbs enervated and heavy. She fought against the feeling.

She loved him more than anything in the world— yes, even more than her art. But no way was she going to let him see that, because she could tell he wasn't here to confess his love for her.

"Well, am I invited in?" he drawled.

Chapter Twelve

She took a deep breath. "Of course, come in." Her voice sounded almost calm.

"Thanks."

In the narrow confines of the hall he was only inches away from her. His breath caressed her face, and the familiar smell of his aftershave created a need to reach up and touch him. At last, after two long weeks, he was here. But being this close to him threatened to choke off her breathing and she slipped past him into the living room. He followed.

She could swear his eyes burned a hole in her back.

At a loss how to proceed with this surprise visit, she made sure the distance between them was the maximum available in the small living room.

"Do I get to sit, or do you prefer we stand here?" Michael's low, smooth voice washed over her. She'd always loved his voice, although now it sounded almost intimidating.

This definitely was not a friendly visit. What did he want from her? She wanted to yell out the question, but instead she gestured toward the couch. "Suit yourself."

But he didn't sit, and instead stood looking around

the room. His eyes fixed on the empty hook and nail on the back wall.

"So, is this where that famous painting hung? Or should I say infamous? The one you took to class for Miguel to see?"

The sarcasm in his voice revealed the purpose of his visit. It seemed Miguel had told him about her bringing the painting to class. Probably then he also knew she'd taken her art to Max. But what made him think he had any right to hassle her about it? It was her painting after all, and it was up to her to decide what she wanted to do with it.

If he truly cared about her art, he should have been happy for her.

"Yes, my painting hung there," she said, trying to put a lid on her growing anger and not sound defensive. "And yes, I took it to class when Miguel asked me to. I also took my work to your friend, Max Storm. But since it's obvious you already know all this, why are you asking?"

"Just making sure I have the facts straight." He flopped heavily onto the couch. "So how come you didn't happen to mention that painting to me? Hmm?"

His eyes never left her, as though he wanted this way to hold her prisoner, perhaps even to punish her.

Shaylee sat on the edge of the armchair, unprepared for this kind of attack, not ready to do battle with him. All this time she'd been nursing her own hurt, what *he'd* done and what *he'd* said. Or left unsaid. And here he was, behaving like he was a judge about to pass sentence on her for something she'd done wrong.

"I just—"

But Michael didn't let her finish. "I must confess it

was quite a surprise when Miguel told me about the painting." Although the words sounded nonchalant, his voice was ominously cold and flat.

"I would've told you about it, after—" Shaylee began, but he cut her off again.

"Yeah? When? In a nice little invitation to your show?" His anger now percolated through the forced calmness.

"I said I would've told you after—."

"After you first told Miguel? Rather than first telling me, your teacher? I don't know why, but I find that a bit disloyal." Cold lasers from his eyes shot straight into her heart. "You can imagine it made me feel a touch foolish to hear Miguel brag to me about it."

Suddenly Shaylee understood how he may have felt at that moment. The revelation must have hurt him, or his pride in any case, and she could even feel a bit sorry for him.

"It wasn't my intention to bring it to Miguel," she said. "But when he asked me to—"

"Naturally. Funny you never mentioned it to me, though."

Shaylee's anger took another spike. "Please stop interrupting me," she fired at him. "I said he *asked* me to bring it."

"Yes, he asked. But how did he know about it in the first place? You must have told him about it, right? Or am I missing a detail here?"

Shaylee glared at him. Michael's caustic voice grated on her ears and a tight, angry knot pressed against her ribcage. He wasn't listening to a word she was saying.

"Marita told him."

"Oh, now it's Marita's fault, is it?"

Shaylee jumped out of her chair. "It's no one's fault, Michael," she cried. "And I have no idea why you came here tonight. If your purpose was to razz me about my painting, I don't want to hear it. This whole affair has *nothing* to do with you. But if you have something else you want to get off your chest, I wish you had phoned me about it."

Michael shook his head. "No, that wouldn't have cut it." His smile was like a cold sneer. "You see, I wanted to make up for the fact that you weren't in Montréal to see how my jaw dropped when Miguel told me about your painting. You would have laughed. Thunk! Michael's jaw hits the floor. Star pupil of Michael Merrick is now the protégée of Miguel Cordova."

"Star pupil?" Shaylee's voice rose to a higher pitch and her hands clenched into tight fists. "How am I suddenly your star pupil? You never called me that. And as for being anyone's protégée, well," she raised her chin haughtily, "I am Shaylee Palmer, *not* your Eliza Doolittle, whom you were going to mentor and then show off as your creation. I did that painting all by myself. And all the rest of them, too. I don't need you to be my Henry Higgins."

Surprise flashed across Michael's face. "What?"

Now she could almost see his jaw dropping.

"Yes, Miguel told me about that ridiculous Eliza Doolittle idea of yours," she shot out angrily.

"I've never said anything about Eliza Doolittle," Michael ground out through gritted teeth. "It was Miguel's stupid idea. I only tried to do what I thought was best for you."

Fury bubbled inside her, but she was able to keep her voice quiet and even. "Sure you did. Like when you told me in the park you could be my mentor and help me become something great. The only thing you were after was showing me off as *your creation* as a feather in your cap."

Michael groaned and raked a hand through his hair. "For God's sake, I never meant it like that. I was honestly trying to help you."

It looked like the tables had turned. Shaylee sat back and clasped her hands. "Michael, I'm not anyone's protégée." Her anger had suddenly evaporated. "I'm just myself, as I've always been."

"As you've *always* been?" Somehow her choice of words had the opposite effect from what she had intended. His arm shot out and angrily he flung a magazine off the couch. "Like you've always known how to paint," he stormed. "If you've *always* been that good, I don't understand why you signed up for lessons and pretended to be a beginner. What a laugh." But the sound that accompanied his words sounded more like an angry snort.

Touché. Shaylee found herself blushing. Yes, she hadn't played totally fair with him, but how could she have told him about her dreams? About her fears and insecurities? A person didn't register for an art class and say to the teacher, "Oh, by the way, actually I'm here to show you how well I can paint, so you'll tell me I'm fabulous." How presumptuous would *that* have sounded?

She sighed in resignation. "Michael, I needed to pluck up my courage before I showed you my painting." She held out a hand, palm up, in an appeal for his understanding. "You never told me my work was any good, and I was too unsure of myself. I *couldn't* show my paintings to someone like you, a famous artist who knows what really good art is. I didn't want to hear you say mine was only *nice*. Can you understand?"

"Of course I understand," Michael shot back. "I went through the same thing myself. I was too *scared* to show my paintings to anyone for fear they'd be laughed right off the easels." His face twitched. "Yes, you heard me right. I was *scared*." He lowered his head so she no longer saw his eyes. "But I showed them to *you*, didn't I?" These words came out in a cracked whisper.

Shaylee froze. Never in a million years had she considered he might be facing the same fears as she.

"But . . . but you already were an accomplished and recognized artist," she protested. "You knew you were good, while I didn't know *what* I was. You'd already proven yourself, but I didn't know if I had what it takes. I was scared to let you see my paintings in case you'd tell me they weren't any good."

"The real issue here is I trusted you, and showed you my lousy art, but you chose to trust Miguel instead." Michael's voice was hard. "I don't mind confessing I was slightly disappointed."

It was obvious her words failed to penetrate through his pain. He wasn't sympathetic to her fears and doubts. "I'm sorry you feel that way," she said quietly. "I honestly didn't mean to hurt you by my actions."

"Hurt me? Hey, don't you worry about me." Michael's voice was rough. Too loud. "I'm okay. I was just curious why you did what you did. But, hey, Miguel's a nice guy." His blasé tone annoyed her.

"Yes, he is," she said defiantly. "He's very nice, and he made me feel like my work was worthy of recognition. And he didn't want to use me like you did. You've always looked out for yourself, disregarding the feelings of others. Like the women in class whom you've been using for your own pleasure. And when you wanted me to go to Europe with you as your Muse, it was to serve *your* needs. You're a selfish, self-centered Henry Higgins."

Shaylee had now more than regained her voice. She couldn't shut off the flow of words. "You've got your nerve, coming here, quizzing me about my painting and behaving like I'd done something wrong. *I'm* the injured party here, don't you forget. *I'm* the one who should be raging at you, for your selfishness. For hurting me."

Michael didn't reply, but his face reddened with anger. "Well, if I hurt you, it's a good thing Miguel is stepping up to soothe the pain. I hope you two will have a great time preparing for the show." He sounded churlish. "Or whatever else you may be doing."

Shaylee stared at him in disbelief. Was he jealous of Miguel? "Michael, there's nothing between Miguel and me."

"How do I know that?" He scoffed. "But I must admit I found this innocent Fairy of the Field act of yours very believable. Call me naïve, call me gullible, but it strikes me as hilarious how you pretended not to be good with watercolours. And not even good at throwing snowballs."

"Snowballs?" Shaylee's laugh came out in an incredulous squeak. "What on earth have snowballs got to do with this?"

"You told me you couldn't hit . . . ah, forget it. It's simply another example of your duplicity."

Anger bubbled out of her. "Michael, you better leave. It's obvious we're just digging ourselves deeper into this horrible quagmire."

He got up and followed her to the door. Standing stiffly she held it open for him. But as he brushed against her in the narrow hall, he suddenly seized her arm and swung her around to face him.

She struggled against him, but he gripped both her arms and held her while she stared up at him in shock and surprise. He lowered his head and then his lips were hard against hers, punishing her with his mouth, eliciting a squeal of protest from her.

But as he continued to kiss her, her arms crept around his neck as though of their own volition, and she yielded and softened against him.

"Shaylee . . ." he whispered against her neck.

For a brief moment she buried her face against his shoulder before she looked up, tears blurring her eyes.

"You'd better leave, Michael," she whispered. "I can't take any more of this."

Miguel and Michael worked in silence in their mutual office. After their bitter exchange over the phone, Michael had been avoiding like the plague any mention of Shaylee or the art show. Not that he cared one way or the other, but from what he'd overheard, he'd been able to figure out things were proceeding smoothly according to plan.

This day was as silent as all the preceding ones had been. But despite the peaceful, albeit strained atmosphere, it was impossible for him to concentrate on anything. He had to keep fighting against the recurring image of Shaylee as he had left her standing at her door.

Going to see her had been stupid, and he should have known, with the anger and disappointment raging inside him, that it would only lead to a terrible confrontation. Though that's exactly why he'd gone. He'd wanted to let her see exactly how her actions had hurt him. He'd been burning for days, and had mistakenly thought he could quench the angry flames with angry words.

But as he'd brushed past her on his way out, something had shattered inside him. Under the hall lamp her violet eyes had burned into him, draining away all the anger, and he couldn't stop himself from kissing her.

And then he'd turned and left. Probably the wisest thing he'd done that day. There was nothing left for either of them to say. Rehashing their differences wasn't getting them anywhere. And although every fiber in his body had told him to turn around and shout out his love for her, he'd forced his feet to keep walking away from her.

What a damned fool he was! Why couldn't he have told her he loved her? Because after the way he'd behaved, accusing her of duplicity, why would she ever want to have anything to do with him. His behaviour was downright despicable. Below the belt.

"So, do you remember what time Mika's flight gets in next week?" Miguel asked, breaking the silence.

Michael refused to be drawn in by the other's conciliatory tone. "It's marked on the calendar," he growled.

Miguel coughed. "Listen, Mike, I wanted to talk to you about Shaylee," he began, but Michael found a reason to walk out of the studio, into the kitchenette.

Miguel followed, crowding into the tiny space. "I met Shaylee yesterday and she asked how you were doing."

"That's nice." Michael brushed past Miguel with a piece of cheese in his hand. He stuffed it into his mouth, muffling his next words. "And you told her I'm doing fine."

Miguel's answer sent an angry shock through him.

"No. As a matter of fact, I told her you're being a huge pain in the ass and a miserable, moping grump."

"You told her *what*?" Michael yelled. "You had no right to say anything like that. I'm doing just fine."

"Like hell you are."

Michael returned to his drafting table. Of course Miguel was right, but Michael wasn't about to admit that. Except maybe to himself. A huge hole had set up permanent residence in his gut and it hurt like hell. He missed Shaylee with every fibre of his body.

"Actually, I've been meaning to talk to you about Sh . . . her myself," Michael said, not looking up from his work. Even saying her name aloud made him bleed. He'd tried it at home, by himself, and had ended up shouting it, raging at the silent walls, as if that would bring her back. Idiotic.

"Yes? What about her?" Miguel lowered his pencil, ready to listen.

"I just wanted to tell you I'm not taking her back as a student when I return from Europe. Not after the way she balked at my instruction, practically staging a revolt in class. I assume she'll register this fall when you're teaching, so she's all yours." All stupid, face-saving talk. He would take her back in a heartbeat if only she were willing to come.

"I see."

Michael didn't like the smile that played around Miguel's mouth when he said that.

"No, you don't see. You don't see a damn thing, Cor-dova."

No one could see he was beating himself up for hav-

ing driven her away with his behavior. Or that he loved
her and wanted her back. Or that dreams of her kept
chasing away his sleep. He'd wake up, thinking she
was there beside him, but she never was. A groan rose
from deep in his chest and he tried to pass it off as a
cough, hoping Miguel hadn't noticed.

"In case you're worried about stepping on my toes,"
Michael continued, "I'm letting you know that as far
as I'm concerned, she's off my radar." He played with
the ruler, sawing it on the edge of the drawing board,
as if attempting to cut her out of his life. "You remember how things were when Ashley left? I moaned and
groaned for a while like the world had ended. But it
didn't. And I'll get over this, too."

"I didn't know there was anything to get over,"
Miguel pointed out with irritating logic. "From what
you've been telling me, you never were interested in
her as anything but a student."

"That's correct. I wasn't," Michael said firmly. "I'm
leaving for Europe and that's that. And I wouldn't take
her along with me even if I wanted. I mean, even if she
wanted . . ." He stopped, confused. "Whatever. So theoretically we're finished even before we start."

"Theoretically?" Again that sardonic smile played on
Miguel's lips. "As opposed to what?"

"As opposed to how things stand." As opposed to
how he needed her back to fill the emptiness that
gnawed at him. Nothing theoretical about that.

In the days since their last meeting, he'd gone
downtown several times and waited among the lunch-
hour crowds, hoping a glimpse of her would ease the
ache inside him. But she hadn't appeared. And each
time he returned to his studio, missing her even more.

"You're not making one iota of sense, Michael. But

I assume you're trying to tell me it's over. Is that how things stand?"

"That's how they stand."

Miguel didn't look convinced, but Michael was relieved he didn't press the issue.

"And for the sake of our business relationship, until I leave for Europe, I'd appreciate it if we did not mention her, or Max, or the show," he said. "If you don't mind."

"I don't mind," Miguel agreed. "But would you mind if I asked her out?"

"Do what you bloody well please!" Michael roared. "Why the hell are you asking *my* permission? I'm not her father. Or one of her dozen brothers." He slammed the ruler on the edge of the drawing board and it broke with the loud crack of a pistol shot.

"That's my ruler," Miguel observed dryly.

Michael tossed the pieces by Miguel's table. "Take it." That confirmed it. Miguel was ready to make his moves on Shaylee. Not only steal Michael's role as her teacher, but take his place in her heart, too. As if he still had a place there.

Casually Miguel picked up the ruler pieces. "Unless, of course, you happen to be in love with her yourself?"

"No!" The word exploded out of Michael. Yes, he was. Madly in love with her. He'd taken such care not to get involved, done his best to prevent her from crawling into his heart and into his very soul. But he'd failed. Completely.

The memory of their precious moments together fired up his blood and Michael turned back to his work, away from Miguel's probing eyes.

"Look, Michael," Miguel said, his voice placating. "I was pulling your leg now with that dating stuff. I'm trying to get you to admit how you really feel about her, but you're obviously too bullheaded."

Michael glowered at Miguel from under his brows, but Miguel ignored him and went on. "Let me ask you something. Haven't you seen the difference in your art since she came on the scene? I have. Which makes me think she's important to you in more ways than you realize."

Defeated at last, Michael leaned his forehead on his hand. "Yeah. I know."

Yes, she was important to him. Not only because she'd helped him get his painting back on track, but because she was . . . Shaylee. Because of all her wonderful qualities. For her sense of fun, her stubbornness, her ability to see beauty in everything around her, her talent, her commitment to her art. And for loving him, a selfish, self-centered Henry Higgins. Yeah, she'd called it right.

If only he hadn't been so blind, so absorbed in his own wants. If only he'd seen the precious gift she offered him.

And if only he had responded to it.

If she would take him back he would gladly commit himself to this love. Shaylee was the most important thing in his life. Yes, even more important than his art. More important than the very air around him. What an idiot he was.

How hurt Shaylee must have been when he didn't respond to her confession of love at Edwards Gardens. His heart had shouted her name and urged him to run after her, but his brain had asked, "And then what? You want to be stuck?"

Her words had surprised him and he hadn't been prepared for them. Hadn't known how to respond. So, like a coward, he'd taken the easy way out and said nothing.

And now he couldn't imagine her ever wanting to speak to him again, especially after his award-winning performance in her apartment.

He sat on the stool, unable to make his eyes focus on the blurred drawing.

Shaylee smiled as she looked at Max Storm's ruddy, beaming face. He stood by the entrance of The Four Winds Gallery, greeting his guests who were arriving for the show. For a change the air in the city wasn't humid and the glass doors were flung open to let in the slight evening breeze blowing up from the lake. On tables covered with white damask the hors d'oeuvres were disappearing quickly and happy chatter bubbled like the champagne that flowed generously tonight.

Shaylee saw that Max fairly bubbled, too, as his "Troika of Rising Stars" mingled with the guests. And although her heart wasn't totally in it, she tried her best to do her part. There was the sculptor, Johanna Meyer, whose sleek, seductive works had gathered a crowd of admirers around her. She was downright seductive herself with her long, raven-black hair, and her rake-thin body sheathed in a figure-hugging black dress. As she talked, her milky, bare arms floated in fluid motions around the sculptures.

And there was Richard Korpi, the tall blond "Viking", as Max called the photographer. Originally from Finland, he now made his home in the picturesque hills of Caledon. Newspapers had written about his striking photos in black and white, with their clever interplay of light and shadow, which challenged the viewers' ideas of what reality was. Yes, he was an obvious hit with the visitors, Shaylee observed, and especially with the ladies who milled around him.

Max gave Shaylee the thumbs-up sign and looked at her with obvious admiration. She smiled and gave a little wave in return, silently thanking him again for giving her this opportunity of a lifetime. He'd called her his "Jewel in the Crown", a title she'd pooh-poohed, but couldn't help being secretly pleased about.

How she'd ever gathered up the pluck to march into his gallery that day, nervously clutching her paintings. She'd tried so hard to appear urbane, but of course Max had seen through her facade. She was surprised he had recognized her as the woman in the clunky boots who had visited his gallery in March.

Max had been "enchanted" by her paintings. "They're so like you," he'd mused. "At first glance they appeared comfortingly familiar, like some scene from my childhood. But as I looked, they bewitched me and began to draw me deep into other, mysterious milieux."

That's what the newspapers had said about them, too. Shaylee smiled to think they probably had taken their text right from Max's enthusiastic mouth. And because of his hype, many of her paintings already held that welcome little red dot, indicating several people had put their money where their admiring mouths were.

For the hundredth time that evening, Shaylee scanned the room. No. She was *not* looking for anyone in particular. Many fans were already vying for her attention, and she did her best to field questions and receive accolades as she stood in their midst.

Miguel was there beside her, but she didn't need his support. This was *her* night, and she'd been trying in vain to nudge him off to join Marita, who was throwing covert glances at him, while chatting with Max.

Her parents had driven up for the opening and now stood hugging the wall, looking totally bewildered, gripping their plates of hors d'oeuvres. Daddy in his dark suit, at least three decades old, and Mum in her best black dress she wore only to weddings and funerals. Shaylee caught their attention and gave a little wave and an encouraging smile. They still didn't seem to quite understand what this celebration was all about, and Shaylee could only guess what went through their minds right now. "Little Doodle-bug Shaylee was actually selling her paintings? Could Grandfather have been right after all?"

Her seven brothers, some with wives and some single, were also present. They stood around in a tight-knit group, obviously out of their element, nibbling delicately at the finger foods, trying to appear like they knew which side was up. They seemed almost puzzled by the comments people were making about their little sister. "What's so big about Shaylee's 'pitchurs'?" their faces seemed to say.

But Shaylee drank it all in, and it went to her head like the brandy had done once, long ago last spring. She looked around her again. Okay, she might as well admit it, she was still hoping Michael would show up. Just seeing him here would turn this day from fabulous to heavenly.

She had also invited her classmates—only Peggy had declined to come—and she smiled as she looked at Britney, in the company of Sue and Helena, discussing photography with tall, blond Richard Korpi. Tracy and Pauline, giggling into their champagne, had told her earlier they were tickled pink to be mingling with real artists like Richard and Johanna. And there stood Bruce and Burt, their plates heaped with food, chatting and pointing with their pinky-fingers at some subtle detail in one of Johanna's sculptures.

Everyone was here, except . . . Shaylee struggled to keep her smile from wobbling. But then well-wishers once again engulfed her, wanting to hear her comments about a particular painting of hers. Everyone was so kind. Nothing but praise had been heaped on her all evening, and the fact that people were actually buying her work for unbelievable sums made Shaylee almost embarrassed.

It *was* a great evening, even if one crucial element was missing.

"Excuse me, Miss Palmer?"

An elderly gentleman stood beside her.

"Mr. Crawley!"

"Yes. I heard about the show and wanted to come and offer my congratulations to my former pupil," her former teacher said. "I am very proud of you, Miss Palmer." He shifted his cane to the crook of his arm and gave Shaylee a solemn handshake that left her speechless. Her old nemesis was congratulating her!

Finally she found her voice. "Thank you, Mr. Crawley."

"I always knew you had it in you," the old gentleman went on. "I was very disappointed when you decided not to continue taking art past the first semester. You had great potential, you know."

"N-no, I didn't know," Shaylee stammered. "I thought . . . I *hoped* maybe I did, but—"

"Well, this certainly proves I was right," Mr. Crawley said with a tinge of smugness, looking around the room at her paintings. He sighed. "If only you had been patient and stayed with it. You had wonderful ability, but you were always so impetuous, wanting to do things your way." He stopped, and for a moment he appeared deep in thought. "But maybe for you that was the right way to proceed and my way of teaching did not suit you. Too old-fashioned, perhaps?"

That's what she'd been telling everyone all these years, even calling him a fossil in her youthful arrogance. "I was such a brat in class." With a rueful smile Shaylee gave her head a shake. "I'm so sorry, Mr. Crawley."

"Yes." Mr. Crawley returned her smile. "You certainly were a challenge at times. But in the end," once more he looked around at her paintings, "in the end things have worked out for the best. I am delighted on your behalf. Congratulations, again, Miss Palmer."

He held Shaylee's hand warmly in both of his and then took his leave in a most polite manner. He was so like his old self that nostalgia overcame her and tears blurred her vision as she smiled at his dignified back.

But no, Mr. Crawley, things hadn't worked out for the best. Things would never be the best for her without Michael.

Chapter Thirteen

Michael stepped in through the open glass doors of
the gallery and immediately looked around, trying to
see through the milling crowds. No, he wasn't looking
for her. Uh-uh. He was only curious to see who all had
shown up for the gala. The food and drink certainly
had drawn people like wasps. And the art, of course.

With so many bodies crammed into the large foyer,
at first he had trouble finding any familiar faces. Then
he saw Marita, but she was busy talking with Max and
didn't notice Michael's brief salute.

He wandered on, trying in vain to keep his eyes from
actively searching for Shaylee. The reason he'd come
was to see her paintings because he was curious why
Max had insisted on including them in this show. He
expected them to be good, but still he wanted to see
for himself.

He stopped in front of one. Yes, it certainly was well
executed and delightful, as her work always was, and
he easily recognized her delicate style. He continued
to stare. Remarkably fine, fresh work. Joyfully enig-
matic. The longer he gazed at the scene, the more be-
guiled he became by some strange aspect he couldn't
put a finger on. The familiar scene invited him to look

deeper at some unexplored, alluring plane that held a promise of untold pleasures, if only he dared to enter. Unexpectedly, the softly swirling clouds gave him a glimpse of his own childhood and left him shaken.

He moved to the next painting. The same thing happened. After looking for a while at the scene that resembled someplace he'd been to as a kid, he found its simplicity deceiving. New visions he had at first failed to notice leaped at him. Something excitingly mysterious pulled him like a magnet into a seductive zone.

Michael gave his head a shake to clear it. The woman was unreal. What had possessed him to think he could guide her and help her become something more than what she already was? Yes, her style was delicate. Why had he thought she should change anything with shadings or splashes of colour? The paintings were perfect. Just the way they were.

And he remembered what Shaylee had said to him. "I'm not your Eliza Doolittle whom you can mentor and then show off as your creation." She was right. He *had* behaved like some arrogant Henry Higgins, planning to bring her out and show the world his great new protégée. He'd been thinking of himself, rather than concentrating on discovering the true magic in her work.

If only she had shown him these paintings, he would have known what a jewel he had in his hands. Not someone with remarkable ability, but a woman with a precious gift. And as for him, he'd failed totally as a teacher, not being perceptive enough to see her lack of self-confidence. Foolishly he'd thought she was trying to elicit flattery from him, and had refused to go along. He should have known Shaylee wasn't like that.

He'd fought so hard against his attraction for her, to the point of sometimes being brusque with her in class, hoping that would prevent her from stealing his heart. But obviously it had been in vain because, in spite of everything, she'd grabbed it and run away with it.

His now heart gave a painful lurch. There she was, almost in front of him, a confident, alluring young woman, smashingly attractive in a simple dress of some soft, violet stuff that shimmered as it softly draped her slim body. The colour accentuated her eyes, and she positively glowed, standing there among her admirers.

And there was Miguel, hovering close beside her, his hand resting on her shoulder. The sight made Michael's hands curl into fists.

The ache that had filled him since they last parted, now turned into a deep, black sorrow. She looked so radiant and so incredibly beautiful as she chatted happily with the people around her, he couldn't face meeting her, not with Miguel there, smiling smugly. Because then he might do something stupid, like punch his friend in the face, pick up Shaylee, kicking and screaming, and carry her away like a grunting caveman.

He turned to make his way back toward the door.

Shaylee felt the familiar tingle at the back of her neck and turned as if in a dream. Through an opening in the crowd, she saw Michael's back as he headed toward the exit. The space closed in and she lost sight of him.

"Michael!" she cried, but her voice was drowned by the din of conversation and laughter. With a quick apology, she broke away from the couple she'd been chatting with and ran after him.

"Michael!" she called again. She jostled people in her

hurry, uttered her excuses, and continued to push ahead. Because of her size, she could see no farther than the backs of the people who stood in her path, but she hoped she was heading in the right direction.

"Please excuse me," she muttered for the tenth time, as she bumped into another back. But this time it was the one she'd been chasing.

"Michael, where are you going?" she asked breathlessly.

At the sound of her voice he turned. Her heart stopped cold at the sight of his gaunt face. Had he been ill?

She placed a hand on his arm to ensure he wouldn't disappear. "I didn't know you were here. Were you going to leave without even speaking to me?" It felt wonderful just to touch him again.

"I would've come to see you, but you were so busy with everyone. With Miguel. I didn't want to interrupt." His voice was wooden. "I saw your paintings. They're fabulous."

His words jolted her heart back to life. "I'm so glad you think they're good. I thought maybe you wouldn't like them." She ignored his comment about Miguel.

He frowned. "Why wouldn't I like them? Anyone with half an eye can see they're wonderful."

"In class you always said my work was too delicate. You wanted me to use—" she smiled impishly, "more Sepia."

People were pushing between them, making it difficult to stay together. Michael took her arm and led her to a corner, placing himself between her and the jostling crowds.

With one hand he braced himself against the wall, and bent his head to hear her better. Shaylee felt totally engulfed by his presence. Being so near to him, she felt she'd died and gone to heaven, but the current that sparked between them told her she was exquisitely, vibrantly alive.

"Now, what were you saying?" he asked with a crooked grin. "About Sepia?" His breath caressed her cheek, and she yearned to reach up and touch his face.

She didn't want to talk about Sepia. She wanted to be in his arms. "It's just that in class you always seemed to find fault with what I'd done." Her legs were beginning to wobble and she glued her palms against the wall behind her for support.

"Always?" His tightly drawn brows told her he'd had no such intent. "I don't think I *always* did. But I guess I didn't praise you too much either, did I?"

She shook her head. "No. That you certainly did *not* do."

"I guess I figured you knew you were good, and were looking for flattery and adulation. I didn't want to make your head swell by praising you too much."

Shaylee gave a short, incredulous burst of laughter. "Praise me too much? Michael, you know your praises never went beyond 'nice'. And I wanted so much to show you my best effort so you would say I was great."

She stopped. If she'd only been upfront with him, instead of letting him think she was a beginner, who knew, maybe all this could have been averted. "But when all I got was 'nice', I felt frustrated and hurt and it made me angry." She sighed. "Maybe that's why I wasn't very receptive to criticism."

Michael affirmed that statement with a nod. "Yes. You argued with me so much it made me feel you didn't trust me as an instructor. I must admit sometimes

I was . . ." He smiled. "Slightly peeved." Then he raised her face so he could look straight into her eyes. "Although this comes much too late, I want you to know I think your art isn't just good. It's fabulous."

Shaylee felt the heat rise to her cheeks as he stroked her chin with his thumb.

"I should have given recognition where it was due," he admitted ruefully.

When he lowered his hand she wanted it back again, caressing her face. She gave a little wicked smile. "Henry Higgins didn't give any praise, either, as I recall."

Michael grabbed her by the shoulders and gave her a shake. "If I hear another word about Henry Higgins . . ." His voice rose above the din, making a few heads turn.

His fingers burned through her light jersey sleeves and the heat threatened to steal away her breath. When he took his hands away, her shoulders felt cold and she wanted him to touch her again. To hold her in his arms, tightly.

"Oops, sorry."

A passerby jostled Michael and pushed him against Shaylee. His face was now so close, his lips so near, she could almost taste them.

And then, incredibly, she could, because after such a long, dry spell they were on hers exactly where they belonged. His arms enclosed her and as his kiss deepened she felt his hunger, as great as her own.

In the hubbub surrounding them, no one but she heard the words she'd been waiting for all her life.

"Shaylee," he murmured hoarsely. "I love you, my darling."

"You love me?" She looked up and scrutinized his

face.

"Yes. Marry me." His breath came out ragged. "Please?"

"But . . . but you don't want any baggage." She spoke against his hammering heart.

"But I do." He took her face in his hands, kissing her again. "I want you, my little baggage, if you'll have me."

At his words a soft giggle bubbled up from inside her. "Michael, I'd love to be your baggage. It's what I want more than anything."

Those golden flecks were once more doing a dance in his eyes and seeing them made her dizzy with happiness. "I love you, Michael," she whispered.

Michael still held her, but loosely enough to look into her eyes. "I've been such a blind, stupid fool about everything. About your art, and mine, too. I never realized that whatever was wrong in my life would reflect in my paintings. Your love helped me get over the cynicism I carried in me. It was your love—yours—that gave my work back its soul." He dug his fingers into her curls. "You know, darling, you came to my class to get reassurance about your painting—which I'm sorry I didn't provide—but ironically, you helped me get my art back on track."

Shaylee gave his cheek a caress. "It was totally unintentional, but I'm glad I did."

"When my paintings started to improve, I must have loved you already, but in my stubborn blindness, I fought against it like crazy." Michael stopped talking long enough to kiss her. "But you stole my heart, you little Fairy of the Field. I'm sure you have some magical powers I'm defenseless against."

Shaylee wanted to believe everything she heard, but

one thing still nibbled at her happiness. She hated to cast doubt into her joy, but she had to ask. "How do you know over time our relationship won't deteriorate like the one you had with Ashley?"

"Because I love you like I've never loved anyone in my life, and I can't think of my life without you," Michael said with such conviction that the clouds of doubt began to dispel.

"And I think we're a great match, you and I, because we have the same goals in life," Michael went on. "We understand each other's dedication to art and we know each of us needs freedom to work. That bond will unite, rather than separate us." His arms went around her again and held her possessively. "We were created for each other."

The sadness that had been threatening to take over her life, now found itself evicted for good.

"These weeks away from you have been the worst," she confessed. "But today is turning into the most wonderful day of my life. More fabulous than I could ever have hoped for in my wildest dreams."

She closed her eyes and rested her cheek against his chest. The pounding of his heart matched hers.

Suddenly Marita's voice broke in through her mist of happiness. "Can you still get her a berth on that ship to Europe, Michael?"

Michael moved off to one side and Shaylee saw that a smiling crowd had formed behind his back. Enthusiastic applause filled the gallery.

In the midst of the happy uproar Shaylee said a silent thank you to her grandfather. His encouragement had made her come to Toronto and now her dream had come true.

Her paintings hung on the walls of an art gallery.

And as icing on the cake, she'd found love.

The fireplace cast a flickering glow into the room as Shaylee and Michael snuggled on the couch in his living room. It was way past midnight, but she was still reeling and dizzy from the successful sale of her work, from Michael's confession of his love for her, from his proposal of marriage and, most of all, from their passionate lovemaking.

She sighed with contentment and leaned her head on his chest. In the foyer of The Four Winds Gallery, when they'd been getting ready to leave, there had been a rather awkward moment. Michael had looked at her with obvious desire, unsure of what she wanted to do.

"Michael," she had told him, "I want to go home with you."

The joy in his eyes had lit up the whole gallery.

Their ardent lovemaking, as soon as they got home, was something Shaylee had only dreamed of just few months ago. Afterwards, they had been too happy and excited to sleep, and now were relaxing in front of the fire. He in his pyjamas and she wrapped in his big terry robe.

Michael rose from the couch. "Time to open the gift from Max." He went to pick up the parcel Max had given them at the gallery as they were leaving. "He said it brought us together," Michael said and handed it to Shaylee.

She ripped open the brown paper wrapping and revealed Michael's winter painting from the gallery.

"Oh, it's so *nice*," she gushed. "Who's the artist?" She pretended to search for the signature. "Michael Merrick? Never heard of him."

"Stop that, you little pixie!" Michael took the painting and placed it on the floor against the wall. "We'll hang it up on the wall, right beside yours." He sat down again and wrapped his arm around her shoulders.

"You know, my first impression was right," Shaylee said. "I thought an artist who could paint a scene as wonderful as this, had to be pretty fabulous himself." She gave him a resounding kiss on the cheek. "And you certainly are." She snuggled back against him. "It's great we're both professional artists now."

"Yeah, it's great," he agreed. "But let me warn you, the feeling of not being good enough never goes away. Probably even your former teacher, the great da Vinci, sometimes felt his work wasn't good enough." He kissed the tip of her nose. "It's just the way we artists are hardwired, I guess."

Shaylee nodded. There was so much about being a professional artist she didn't know yet. But she knew she was on her way. It was inevitable there would be times when life would knock her down, but she would always have Michael's love to strengthen and sustain her. Just as he would have hers.

Michael turned her face up to look at him. "By the way, you did it again, you know." He gave her a dimpled grin.

Shaylee frowned. "Did what?"

"At the gallery, when someone pushed me against you, you raised your lips to mine."

"I did not," she retorted. "You were the one who brought your lips down on mine, and you know it."

"Uh-uh. You were the instigator, just like that first time it happened in the studio."

"No *way*." She slipped out of his arms and tried to

escape, but Michael grabbed her by the waist and swung her down onto his lap.

"All right, woman. Just to show I don't do things like that, I won't kiss you again." He held her pinned against him and nuzzled her neck under her jaw.

"Oh, you shouldn't do that to a simple country girl," she protested in a tremulous whisper.

"My morals forbid me to kiss a simple country girl." He continued his teasing by nibbling her earlobe.

"Morals?" Shaylee snorted. "The closest you've ever been to morals is murals, you Lothario."

He stopped nibbling and looked at her, puzzled. "Lothario?"

"Don't ask."

As desire diffused through her, she melted against him. "All right, I confess. It *was* me. Now kiss me," she whispered.

About Karen Rossi

Karen Rossi (the pen name of Kaarina Brooks) has been a romantic since she was a child. She and her sister had their own "publishing company" and wrote about love-struck princes and princesses.

Today she writes grown-up romances where modern-day "princes and princesses" go through heart-wrenching relationship struggles before reaching their happily ever after.

She now also has a real publishing company, Wisteria Publications. Besides romances, she also publishes kids' books and non-fiction works, such as a cook book.

She lives in Southern Ontario with her husband and kitty-cat, Lilly.

www.wisteriapublications.com
brooks.kaarina@gmail.com